Mind of a Killer
A Scarlett Bell Thriller

Dan Padavona

Copyright Information

Published by Dan Padavona

Visit our website at www.danpadavona.com

Cover Design by Elderlemon Design

Proofreading - Lydia Capuano

Although some of the locations in this book are actual places, the characters and setting are wholly of the author's imagination. Any resemblance between the people in this book and people in the real world is purely coincidental and unintended.

Mind of a Killer - Paperback

Mind of a Killer - Paperback

CHAPTER ONE

The horror movie credits rolled as Kacy Deering took one more sip of gin and pulled Braden's arm off her shoulder. Braden touched her bare thigh and she swatted his hand, softening the gesture with a smile.

"Not now."

"Come on, Kacy."

"What if the Walshes come home?"

The television volume was low so it wouldn't disturb five-year-old Chase upstairs. The hands on the grandfather clock edged closer to eleven. Though the Walshes weren't due back until midnight, Kacy remembered them returning an hour early the last time she babysat. A few minutes earlier and they would have caught Braden sneaking down the driveway in the dark.

The boy moved his hand back to her thigh. She grabbed his wrists with a playful giggle.

"Stop."

He sighed.

"Fine. Be that way."

"It's not like I don't want to."

"Yeah, yeah. But never tonight, always next time."

He pushed himself off the leather sofa and snatched

his sweatshirt. Yanking it over his head, he ripped the keys from his pocket. That was another thing. His Charger was parked in the driveway. Old Clyde Sullivan next door wouldn't notice the car due to the bordering oaks and privacy fence, but he'd hear the thumping bass of the car stereo and see the headlights burning holes into the garage. And if the Walshes happened to pull up…

Kacy brushed the hair from her eyes and folded her arms.

"I'm sorry," she said, looking down at the floor.

"It's not a problem."

The way he glared at the door indicated it most certainly was a problem.

"Call me in the morning. I'll make it up to you soon. I promise."

Braden nodded. Then he was gone into the June night.

Through the closed door she heard the engine gun, followed by music blasting. Something pinged off the undercarriage, probably a rock. Then nothing. Worrying again about Mr. Sullivan, Kacy parted the curtains and stared across the property. Thick foliage cloaked the Sullivan's house.

Just the dark night.

The quiet of the sprawling Dutch Colonial pressed down when she closed the curtains, strangely deafening. Kacy rubbed goosebumps off her arms and turned on the news. Anything to break the silence.

Thump.

She was about to flop onto the couch when the noise scared her. Couldn't discern if it came from upstairs or outside.

"Chase? You awake?"

She turned off the television and listened. No pitter-patter of feet crossing the upstairs hall, no toilet flush or water running.

She called the boy's name again and shrugged when no reply came. Running her eyes across the living room, her heart leaped as she eyed the half-empty bottle of gin on the end table.

"Shit," she said, quickly snatching the bottle and stuffing it into her backpack, wondering how she could be so careless.

Kacy's feet slapped the polished hardwood as she carried their glasses into the kitchen. While she waited for the sink to fill she breathed against her hand. No scent of alcohol. She scrubbed the glasses clean, dried and put them away in the cupboard, the busy work settling her mind. She felt foolish for getting jumpy after watching a horror movie as if she were in middle school again.

Back in the living room she packed her windbreaker and wrapped it around the bottle. Evidence concealed. Now she only had to wait for the Walshes to come home, fingers crossed that the neighbors didn't hear Braden leave.

Thump.

Louder this time, too heavy for a child's footsteps.

Suddenly she was terrified of the Dutch Colonial's hidden corridors, of the night scraping at the windows and how every shadow looked deformed and monstrous.

She padded to the staircase and peered up. Darkness swallowed the second-floor landing.

"Chase? You didn't fall, did you? Chase?"

Little more than a whisper emanated from her dry throat.

Kacy grabbed her phone. Fingers squeezed the case as she held the banister and placed one foot on the bottom stair. Braden would be home in a few minutes. She contemplated calling him, then decided she couldn't deal with him making fun of her for being afraid.

She flicked the wall switch. Now she viewed the top of

the stairway. A fire lily accented the landing, its red petals open like gaping mouths.

Halfway up the stairs she stopped and listened. Perhaps the sound had been the bathroom door slamming.

But the bathroom and bedroom doors were open when Kacy reached the landing, all rooms spilling black shadows into the hallway like blood in the moonlight. She didn't like the twin quarter-moon windows. Like Halloween pumpkin eyes.

Her heart was a trip hammer. It climbed into her throat and constricted her lungs. Kacy knew she was being foolish. Her mind refused to stop racing.

Houses made strange sounds sometimes, but never this loud.

She swiped at the phone and pulled up her contacts. Wanted to phone her mother. And say what? That a bump in the night turned her into a frightened toddler?

Kacy took another measured step down the hall. The floor was chilly on her feet. From this angle, the boy's bed was impossible to see. She carefully edged toward his room, frightened when the floorboards squeaked.

Chase's bedroom was only steps away, yet it seemed so far. Miles away. If only she could break the ice off her legs and move faster. The plan was already firm in her mind—she would go inside, close and lock the door, curl up beside the boy and wait until the Walshes came home. Which should be any minute now.

The floorboards groaned while she was still. Wasn't her. Who—

The light switch flicked off a split second before the landing went black.

A gloved hand covered Kacy's mouth. Suffocated her scream and dragged it under. A slice of moonlight flared across the knife's surface before the intruder raked the blade across her throat.

A terrible burning. Tearing. Choking.

Then she was one with the darkness. Tumbling into the depthless black.

CHAPTER TWO

The shrill of the phone ringing pulled Scarlett Bell out of a deep sleep. The nightmare was back, worse than it had been in years.

Reaching for the phone, she knocked the sleeping pills off the table and spilled her water. It poured onto the carpet as she cursed and righted the glass.

"Bell," she said, turning on the lamp.

"You awake yet?"

She wasn't sure who it was until Neil Gardy's trademark snicker tickled her ear. The laugh was something close to Muttley, a cartoon dog from her childhood, and always managed to lighten her mood. The clock read four, the first grays of predawn bubbling out of the Atlantic and touching the windows.

"I am now."

Grabbing the first thing she saw which passed for a rag, she dropped her t-shirt on the spill and stomped down. The cotton wicked the water and touched the sole of her foot.

"How soon can you be at Dulles?"

Her adrenaline ratcheted up.

"Uh…I don't know." Scarlett fumbled through the

fallen items on the floor and retrieved her wallet and FBI badge. At thirty-two, she was the Behavior Analysis Unit's youngest agent. "Six-thirty if I hurry."

"Make it six."

Opening the sliding glass door, she let the thick humidity caress her skin. The Potomac sparkled below her walk-out deck, the salty taste of the Atlantic on the wind. Inside, she hurriedly stuffed three days worth of shirts and pants into an overnight bag, still no idea how long she'd be away or why she needed to leave.

"What's the rush?"

"Someone murdered a teenage girl in the Finger Lakes."

"New York."

"Right. Tiny village called Coral Lake. Ever hear of it?"

With a huff, Bell realized she'd need socks and underwear and started unloading her dresser drawer.

"Can't say that I have. I don't get it, though. One murdered girl shouldn't require BAU assistance."

"Normally it wouldn't," he said. She heard a zipper, probably Gardy sealing his suitcase, ready to bolt and waiting for her to get moving. "It's not pretty. The girl was babysitting. Our unknown subject slit the girl's throat and chopped her into pieces."

"Jesus." Jillian popped back into her head. The memories always did when a young person was murdered. "Tell me the kids weren't..."

"Only one kid in the house. And, no. He didn't touch the boy. Only the babysitter. Maybe he didn't know the boy was there. Somehow the kid slept through the whole ordeal."

Bell released her breath. Being a sound sleeper might have kept the child alive.

"One more thing." A pause, as if he didn't want to tell her something. It wasn't like Gardy to pull punches. "He scalped her."

"He what?"

"Scalped the skin and hair off her head and took it with him, along with her clothes." She let the bag drop and fell down on the bed. Her head spinned. "You still with me?"

"I'm here," she said, forcing herself into a sitting position as she switched the phone to her other ear. "That's unique to say the least. What does CODIS say? Any similar murders in New York over the last few years?"

"Nothing like that, no. Which tells me one thing. He's new to this."

"And just getting started."

"Exactly. If he's this violent on the first kill, imagine when he escalates." Bell didn't want to imagine. "But we've got to hit the ground running. The murder occurred Friday night so we're already a day-and-a-half behind."

"Why the delay?"

"I don't think the local sheriff knew what he had on his hands. He didn't consider the serial killer possibility. Good thing he realizes he's in over his head. The crime scene techs have been over everything, but the house is undisturbed. Minus the body parts, of course. But the scene gets a little more stale with each lost second, which is why we need to be on that flight."

She did the math in her head. If she settled for a granola bar for breakfast, she could shower and be out the door in forty-five minutes. Then there was the traffic around D.C. to deal with, always a potential fly in the ointment. At least it was a Sunday morning and not a workday.

"Okay, I'll be there by six."

"Before six."

"But you said—"

"Up and at 'em, sunshine. See you in a few."

Typical Gardy. He always wanted things done five minutes ago. Gardy was one of the BAU's most respected agents, a prime candidate for Deputy Director of CIRG, the Critical Incident Response Group. It couldn't happen soon enough as far as Bell was concerned. Anyone was a fitting replacement for Don Weber and his religious devotion to statistics. Bell appreciated someone needed to fight the higher-ups, and statistical proof validating BAU's crime-solving methodology was critical for funding, but did he need to treat everyone like a number?

After showering she raked the brush through her straight, blonde hair. It touched the tops of her shoulders, the longest her hair had been since senior year at George Mason. In the mirror, her emerald eyes appeared to glow under the LED lighting, almost cat-like.

In the quiet of the bathroom the memory of her dream returned. She was nine-years-old again, as was the case each time the dream returned. Fate lent her another opportunity to warn her friend. Don't let Jillian walk home alone. Stay away from the creek. The water was dangerous, and someone had seen a stranger along the banks.

During sleepovers Jillian was always afraid of the dark. When the lights went out Bell would croon like a ghost until Jillian yelped and turned the lights back on. Then the door would open and Mrs. Rossi would be angry, warning Jillian she would wake the neighbors. Then one day someone stole Jillian away and turned the lights off forever.

The abduction and murder remained an open sore for Bell, a wound that would never heal.

Shaking herself out of her thoughts, Bell hurried to the bedroom and dressed, snatched the granola bar out of the cupboard when she finished.

She was packed and running for the door, the .40 caliber Glock-22 holstered, when she remembered the sleeping pills. They rattled in the bottle as she unzipped the overnight bag and stuffed them inside with her clothes, a subtle reminder to make an appointment with her therapist, Dr. Morford, when she returned. Whenever that might be.

The viciousness of the murderer simultaneously terrified and invigorated her, as did the prospect of getting inside his head. Somewhere to the north, the killer walked among his unknowing neighbors, breathing the same air, waiting for an internal alarm to sound and propel him to kill again. Bell's stomach tingled with the excitement of the hunt.

One final glance around the apartment to ensure the oven burners were off and the windows locked, and she shut the door.

She could already see the sun growing out of the horizon when she reached the highway, the distant ocean bloody and frothing.

CHAPTER THREE

The flight into Syracuse was turbulent, the plane dropping and tilting in roller coaster undulations. Gardy looked a little green beside Bell. He kept eyeing the vomit bag.

"So tell me more about the sheriff," Bell said.

She wanted to keep him talking and take his mind off the bumpy ride. The window light brought out flecks of gray in Gardy's eyebrows and short, brown hair.

"Sheriff Lerner. Less than a year on the job and it shows. He's part of a disturbing trend—politicians without law enforcement backgrounds who know a thing or two about winning elections, but not so much about law enforcement."

"You think that's why he didn't call for help sooner?"

"You mean he wanted the spotlight for solving the case on his own."

Gardy paused when the plane tilted, and for a frozen moment Bell felt sure he was about to snatch the bag from the seat compartment and yawn his breakfast. Thankfully the plane steadied.

"No. I don't think he understood the gravity of the situation. In his mind, it was the girl's boyfriend or a former lover with a jealous streak."

"Tell me about the boyfriend."

"Braden Goodrich, age 17. No criminal record, exemplary grades, star attackman on the lacrosse team and headed to Syracuse University."

"Doesn't sound like our target."

"Doesn't mean he didn't do it, either."

Gardy waved at the female flight attendant, who winked and produced a can of ginger ale. He winked back as she handed him the can, and the girl disappeared to the back of the plane with a hint of rosiness on her cheeks.

"Suave."

"I try."

Bell wondered if Gardy really tried. The special agent was in his middle-forties now, unmarried and without a steady girlfriend. Though Bell had only worked beside Gardy for a year, she understood the special agent was married to his job, an admirable trait that would leave him lost and alone when he eventually retired.

"You should ask the girl for her number."

He cocked an eyebrow and grinned.

"Ask for her *number*? That is so yesterday. I'm surprised you didn't suggest I ask what sign she was."

"Sign?"

"You know. Pisces, Capricorn. Her Horoscope sign, ya dig?"

Bell shook her head.

"I don't dig. Must have been before my time, old man."

The plane dipped again, and this time Gardy snatched the bag and stuffed it into his jacket.

"Better safe than sorry." Gardy sipped the drink, then burped into his hand and sighed in relief. "Maybe I'll keep it. These things make great sandwich bags."

She pulled the case file from his open briefcase and spread the photos across her lap. The pretty flight attendant strolled back to Gardy, saw the pictures and quickly retreated to her station.

"Thanks a lot."

"Sorry about that. Don't worry. You'll see her when we disembark. Plenty of time to find out if she's really a Capricorn."

His Muttley laugh told her the nausea was gone as she turned her attention to the pictures, more gory and disturbing than she'd feared. At the bottom of the stack was a year-old photograph of Kacy Deering. The perfect lighting and canned smile marked it as a yearbook photo, a hint of mischievousness in the teenager's eyes. Bell wondered what Kacy's parents must be going through.

The Syracuse airport was tiny and vacant compared to Dulles, the building undergoing a remodel. The dusty air made Bell cough as they carried their bags through the terminal.

Sheriff Lerner was waiting for them outside, his Dodge Ram running curbside. Summer heat glistened the sheriff's brow. He had the stooped appearance of a man who'd been sedentary for too much of his life, belly drooping over belt, knees weary and failing.

"Agents Gardy and Bell?"

Gardy tilted his ID badge, plainly visible around his neck, as was Bell's. He held out his hand and Lerner took it. The sheriff's eyes passed disinterestedly over Bell, dismissing her as though she were Gardy's child on take-your-kid-to-work day.

"Thanks for meeting us."

"Figured it would be quicker if you followed me. The highway won't get you to Coral Lake, but I know a few shortcuts that will. I trust the flight was okay?"

"Not so much."

They followed the sheriff's truck in a rented Accord. The air conditioning was frigid, and the scent of cigarette smoke was burned into the seats. Gardy saw Bell scrunch her nose and nodded.

"Yeah, it's against the rules to smoke in these things," he said, one hand on the steering wheel, eyes shifting between the road and Bell. "It's the maintenance workers. They're always taking drags on their breaks, then they crawl inside the vehicle and bring the stench with them."

It took a half-hour to reach the village of Coral Lake. The water was the first thing to grab Bell's attention. Deeper blue than a clear sky in January. She couldn't take her eyes off all that blue. Foaming waves crested and broke in the wake of a speedboat. Several boats were out on the water, one man casting a fishing line, a couple floating in a canoe. Beside a long pier in the center of town, people lined up for a boat tour.

The village was small and quaint and bursting with money. Interspersed among the eateries were antique shops and pricey clothing stores. The sheriff's brakes flared and Gardy stopped behind him, allowing a parade of affluent-looking villagers to cross the intersection. Across the street, a woman wearing a Bluetooth earpiece exited a Lilly Pulitzer store carrying two shopping bags. Outside a brick homemade ice cream shop, an older man and a young boy accepted ice cream cones through the window, the younger boy tilting the cone and hurriedly licking the melt.

It hardly seemed possible for an active serial killer to be stalking this otherwise idyllic slice of life.

Soon the village center faded in the mirrors, and the sheriff turned onto Coral Hill. Upscale homes amid a dotting of mansions popped out of the trees as the serpentine road curled up a gentle incline. Bell's questions about how the killer butchered Kacy Deering without attracting attention were answered by the designed seclusion of Coral Hill. Privacy fences girded the properties, and most of the homes were set deep into the trees. Another layer of isolation.

Lerner's truck turned up a stone driveway and parked outside a white, looming Dutch Colonial with blue shutters and quarter-moon windows cut into the second story.

Bell leaned her arm out the window.

"Can you see the neighbor's house?"

"No. You'd think this was the only house on the street."

Thumbs in his belt loops, Lerner stood on the porch. A fist-sized chunk of glass was missing on the left side of the Walsh's door. A yellow rope of police tape blocked the entryway and swayed like a jump rope.

Yanking down the tape, Lerner stood aside for the special agents.

"As you can see, the perpetrator broke the glass to gain entry, though nobody heard. The closest neighbor is Clyde Sullivan," Lerner said, gesturing at a dense stand of elms and birch. "If you look close you can see his garage through the trees."

Gardy slipped off his sunglasses.

"Close enough to hear glass shatter."

"Sure, except Mr. Sullivan don't hear too well these days. You could park a semi in his driveway and yank the air horn for an hour before he'd notice."

"Hmm."

Lerner shifted uneasily when the conversation stopped. He didn't know what to do with his hands, which he switched between belt loops and pockets as the special agents glared at him. Then his eyes widened with understanding.

"Oh, yes. You'll be wanting to view the crime scene now. Let me show—"

"That won't be necessary, Sheriff," Bell said, striding past Lerner.

The sheriff glanced at Gardy, a desperate plea for the special agent to intervene.

"She's the boss," Gardy said, smiling. "No worries, Sheriff. We'll take it from here."

CHAPTER FOUR

The interior of the house was chilly from air-conditioned air spilling down the walls. In the foyer, summer heat bled through the broken pane and forced the cooling system to work overtime. The downstairs lighting was a study in contrast, sunshine beaming through the windows while shadows crawled from the corners.

The foyer opened to a sprawling living room, replete with a grandfather clock, gas fireplace, and ceilings which seemed to stretch to the sky. A 60-inch television hung on the wall. To the left was a kitchen accented by a long island. The stairway stood off the foyer.

Bell sat on the couch and jotted down her observations onto a notepad. Taking notes on her phone was more convenient, but Bell strongly believed in the connection between hand and mind when it came to processing information. Behind her, Gardy's footsteps echoed through the downstairs like water drops in a cavern. Though the preliminary investigation indicated no signs of forced entry besides the obvious pane break, the older agent checked each window and door as he scanned for anything the sheriff's department missed. And based on their assessment of Lerner, Bell wouldn't have been surprised to learn they missed plenty.

It was quiet for a while, just the hollow footsteps and the old house slumbering. A hand touched her shoulder and she jumped. Hadn't noticed Gardy coming up behind her.

"Sorry. Didn't mean to sneak up on you." Peering over her shoulder, he glanced at her scribbles. "You need more time before we do the walk-through?"

Bell clicked the pen several times in thought, then she shook her head.

"No, I'm ready."

"Then let's—"

"I need to do this alone, Gardy. Just the first walk-through, then we'll look together."

He opened his mouth to argue and thought better of it. A year together had taught him not to argue or question how she got inside the mind of a killer.

"Then I guess I'll walk the perimeter, check out the backyard."

He waited for affirmation but she was deep in thought, already putting herself in the killer's shoes, seeing the house as he saw it. Gardy sighed and walked away. She never heard the door shut.

Bell tucked the folder and notepad under her arm and climbed the staircase. A cherry wood banister ran the length of the stairs, and a flowering plant bloomed on the second landing.

She took each step slowly, picturing the killer moving in her place. Silent. Stalking. Watching Kacy Deering from the shadows.

That was the first piece of conflicting narrative. Why didn't she hear him shatter the window?

She might have been listening to music. God knows kids turn the volume up to dangerous levels these days, but the investigators didn't find earphones on the landing. Just her phone. And all those body parts. Bell knew he took her clothes as trophies, a way to live out his fantasies. Keep the girl alive in his mind while her parents mourned. Where was he? Close. Not a drifter. A local. Someone everyone knew. Someone who knew Kacy.

A chill touched her on the landing. It wasn't the air conditioning.

A macabre blood spray covered the walls on the second floor, the floorboards black and stained beneath the attack.

Bell's fingers trembled. She could barely hold the folder as she knelt down and spread the photographs across the hardwood. Her breaths flew in-and-out as she studied the pictures, the grisly scene made all too real now that she was at the murder scene.

This was where it happened. Where the killer butchered Kacy.

Chase's bedroom door leaned open. A few toys lay scattered across the floor. Five-year-olds were notoriously heavy sleepers, yet she couldn't believe the boy slept while Kacy screamed outside his doorway. It didn't make sense.

Unless Kacy didn't scream.

Which meant the killer approached from behind. Took her by surprise.

Careful not to mar the evidence, she stood beside the blood splatter, facing Chase's door as Kacy surely had. Perhaps the teenager heard something upstairs, thought it was the boy and came to check on him. Only it wasn't the boy.

Her neck hairs prickled as if someone was behind her.

Bell spun around to an empty hallway. Twin beams of sunlight blazed through the quarter-moon windows. She let out a breath and removed her hand from the Glock's hilt.

The bathroom was to her right, the master bedroom one door down, with a spare room tucked into the corner behind the rail. All the doors hung open.

Stooping down, she lifted Kacy's yearbook photo and

ran her eyes over the girl's face. By now she'd memorized every angle and curve, the exact arc of the teen's smile, the way one eyebrow arched as though she was in on a joke. When Bell finished, she imagined the teenager standing alone in the hallway moments before the murder. Pictured her outside Chase's doorway, back turned to where Bell now stood.

"Where did you watch her from?"

Her voice trembled and cracked.

A wall switch was affixed between the bathroom and bedroom doors. She flipped it up and evened out the harsh beams through the window.

Bell stepped inside the bathroom and closed the door to a sliver opening. Squinting, she craned her neck but couldn't see the murder scene. The door handle was closest to Chase's room, making it impossible for the killer to observe Kacy without ducking his head out. Perhaps the killer hid in secluded darkness before he struck. She didn't think so. No, he'd want to watch the girl, fantasize over the murder first, a twisted foreplay.

The master bedroom offered a better viewing angle of the blood stain, but even with the door cracked open, chandelier lighting flooded inside, casting a spotlight on anyone spying into the hallway. This wasn't the killer's hiding spot.

That left the spare room.

She knew this was the room the minute she stepped inside. Felt his presence like transient heat after the fire burned out. From this vantage point she could hide in shadow and see Chase's door, the chandelier light falling short of the threshold. Taking nothing for granted, she walked the room, hurriedly snapping photos on her phone. Her nerves were hot wires. For the first time since the investigation began, Bell felt she'd picked up his trail. The room appeared undisturbed. One bed stood in the far corner with the bedspread tight as concrete. Unless guests were in town, nobody slept here. A cherry wood dresser stood opposite the bed. She dutifully checked the insides and found nothing.

He might have hidden in the large walk-in closet. This is almost as big as my bedroom, she thought. Empty shelves. A lonely close hanger.

She got down on all fours, the thick pile carpet soft on her knees as she searched for anything that might belong to the killer. Although she found nothing, Bell made it a point to ensure the crime scene techs swept the closet.

Convinced there was nothing else to find, she headed for the doorway. Something caught her eye. An imperfection on the door frame at eye level. A hole.

Initially it looked like a bad patch job after the removal of a hook-and-eye latch. She bent close and turned a penlight on the frame. The splintered shavings told her he'd used a sharp object, almost certainly his knife, to cut into the wood. Bell pictured him alone in the dark. Glaring at the unknowing girl. Anxiously plunging the knife tip into the frame, spinning the weapon with a powerful grip until the blade whittled in.

Her hands were sweaty. The killer *knew* she was on his trail. The sensation was so sudden and powerful that she sprinted across the room and pulled back the blinds. Lerner's truck sat below, the heavyset sheriff leaning against the grille with his arms folded. Her footfalls echoed as she ran down the hallway to Chase's bedroom. Stepping over the spilled toys, she drew back his blinds and peered into the backyard. Nobody in the yard. The trees swayed as though laughing.

"What are you doing?"

She screamed and spun around to Gardy in the doorway. Mottled light turned his face into a picket fence.

"Easy now. You okay?"

Bell willed her breathing to slow.

"Yeah...yeah, I am. Grab Lerner. I know where he

watched her."

CHAPTER FIVE

The vents blow stale, warm air across his face. The van won't cool anymore. The heat makes him nauseous, trickles salty wetness down his forehead.

Inside, everything smells of copper piping and grease like the after-hours scent of a fast food restaurant. Nervous, he plays with the radio dial. It's the news, someone talking about the stock market. Not talking about the murder.

Everyone in the village talks about him, but they don't know he's the killer. Yesterday he replaced the Fenton's water heater, and Mrs. Fenton couldn't stop jabbering over Kacy Deering and the horrible monster who killed her. It was enough to make him laugh inside. Frightened him that she might see the smile creep into his eyes and crawl out of him like a black widow.

He's learned to be patient, and he must be. They are looking for him now. Everyone is. But *they* are, especially.

His gaze falls on the blue Accord. There's a small dent above the rear wheel well. It's not their car, but a rental. These must be the agents, for who else would accompany the sheriff to the Walsh house? His neighbors gossip, and when they talk he learns things. It's a small village, Coral Lake. Everyone knew the agents had arrived as soon as they drove into the main square, hugging close to Sheriff Lerner's Dodge Ram like obedient mutts, passing so close to his front door that he could have personally greeted them from his front stoop.

A trickle of panic runs down his back. Kacy is alone now. Unprotected.

She won't run away, but someone might try to steal her from him. The agents will certainly try.

Last evening he heard a hiker move through the woods and pass close to his personal space. Kacy's new home. He could hear the hiker stomp through brush, the firecracker pops of sticks snapping. The knife was in his hand, its blade sharp and still carrying the girl's scent. He was ready to defend his home, to protect Kacy, before the footsteps receded down the hill and he released his breath.

The sun is a molten glare on the windshield. He grips the steering wheel, squeezes with held breath, knuckles white. He strains until his face reddens, then releases.

The warmth of relaxation caresses his body. It begins at his scalp and works through his arms and legs. A pins-and-needles sensation.

He is brave to be here in full view. Anyone can see the van, but they don't suspect his intentions.

His tension released, he closes his eyes and imagines the shed. One light bulb affixed to the ceiling, powered by a solar panel. Pine scents from surrounding trees coloring the musty mattress smell. Their sanctuary. No one can hurt them there.

He doesn't like to remember the leather straps affixed to the cot and hopes he never has to use them. He doesn't think he will. Kacy accepts him now and may one day learn to love him after she recognizes how he protects her. Yet the straps are a necessary reminder that, if she is disloyal, punishment will be necessary.

The female agent's shadow passes over the upstairs window in the Walsh house. The spare room. She must feel his presence by now, senses him behind corners and in every shadow. She fears him. This makes him smile. He cannot see her face because the house is much darker than the midday sun. Only the hint of a silhouette. A specter in the glass. The male agent enters the house. Earlier he observed the agent paw around the property and considered entering the house while the man was in the backyard. It would have been so easy to kill the sheriff. Leave him bleeding behind the truck. Then he would edge the front door open, careful not to step upon broken glass and give himself away. Ascend the stairs.

Movement in the driveway catches his eye. Then he sees her and his heart freezes. The female agent.

She is more beautiful than he dreamed. Blonde hair that catches the light. Soft, red lips. He watches her move animatedly between the sheriff and the male agent, can't hear what she's saying but knows it's about him. And Kacy.

He thinks the beautiful agent deserves the opportunity to meet Kacy in person, to come live with them and understand his only desire is to keep them safe.

"Why did I ever agree to let such a disgusting boy into my home?"

The woman's voice makes him jump. His neck burns red where the seatbelt bites and pulls him down.

Pulse racing, he ensures the windows are still rolled up. Prays nobody heard the voice.

In the mirror, he spies the long metal trunk in the back of the van. Chains hooked to each side because it slides easily. She shouldn't be able to talk inside the trunk, and this troubles him. At least she cannot hurt him anymore, not locked away. Does she know about Kacy?

"Answer me, filthy child."

He opens his mouth to answer and nothing comes out. His throat is too dry. Heart climbs into his voice box and pounds.

His eyes lock on the mirrored image of the trunk.

Somehow he feels safer watching the trunk through the mirror, as though spinning around to look directly at the case will cause the chains to snap apart and the top to fly open. Releasing her fury upon the world.

"M…mother."

No reply. The tension rises inside the van.

"What do you want? Well, just don't sit there with your tongue tied into knots. Say something. Or are you too simple to speak?"

He checks the side mirrors. None of the neighbors are on the road. Yet she is too loud. Someone will hear.

"Answer me!"

He swallows. For a moment, he sees the male agent's head shoot up and look in his direction. They shouldn't be able to see him through the tinted windows from this far away.

After a pause, the male agent rejoins the conversation.

As static pops from the AM radio, he begins to speak, shy and fearful initially before his confidence grows. Though she may scream, he holds the power now.

He tells Mother of his job and the many people he meets every day. Yes, he speaks freely with them, no longer feels the need to cower in the presence of others. The village respects him. He does not share with her his secret activities. She won't approve and will yell again, and then the agents will hear.

When she doesn't snap back at him, he continues with more conviction. He has a girlfriend. Yes, really. She is a very pretty girl, kind of heart and loyal. The words aren't out of his mouth for more than a moment before he regrets them, wishes to pull them back. He braces himself, expecting Mother to demand he introduce Kacy to her.

Kacy. He must remember not to speak her name aloud, lest Mother learn her identity and seek her out.

At that moment, the female agent climbs into the Accord. While Mother tells him to continue, to tell her more about his new girlfriend, he waits for the male agent to join the woman. He doesn't. Instead, he pulls himself up into Sheriff Lerner's truck. The Ram's engine growls, brake lights burning like hateful eyes. Like Mother's eyes.

A cloud of dust kicks up as the truck speeds down Coral Hill. It winds around curves, and then he cannot see it anymore.

Now it is just the beautiful woman in the Accord. Alone in the driveway where he'd waited in darkness with the house key.

He clears his throat.

"And there is another woman, Mother."

Yes, another woman. The beautiful agent. She could learn to love him, too.

CHAPTER SIX

Gardy and Bell split up to save time on their interviews. While Bell headed to the Deering house, Lerner drove Gardy into the village center.

Bathed in sunlight, the Coral Lake Suites stood on the lake shore, radiant and stately. There was no lobby to speak of in the boutique resort, just a hallway which led to three first-floor suites. Guests picked up keys at a sister resort down the road, Lerner had told him before wandering across the street to the cafe. An elevator gave access to the second and third floors. The Walshes were checked into 301.

The elevator stopped on the second floor, and an older woman in flip-flops and a sunbonnet stepped inside and pressed the button for the lowest floor. When the car moved again, she smiled and put a hand over her mouth.

"Oh, dear. I thought it was going down."

"No worries. It'll get you there eventually."

Her eyes fluttered about the elevator, the woman obviously uncomfortable locked inside an elevator car with a complete stranger until she noticed his badge.

"You must be the agent everyone is talking about."

"Ma'am?"

"The FBI person."

He snickered.

"Agent Gardy. And I'm not alone."

"Two agents?"

"Yes."

"My goodness. Two secret agents in Coral Lake. It doesn't seem possible."

"We're not secret agents, ma'am," Gardy said, trying hard not to double over laughing. Already he could feel his chest tickle. "My partner and I work for the Behavior Analysis Unit."

The woman gasped.

"You mean like that show on television? The one where they hunt for serial killers every week?"

Gardy's shoulders shook.

"Something like that, yes."

"Candice Squires," she said, offering her hand.

"Neil Gardy. But I suppose you can see that from this unfortunate badge."

She waved her curiosity away and shook her head.

"I'm terribly sorry for being nosy. It's just that..." She looked down, the light gone from her eyes. "It's so awful what happened to that girl. She was a senior in high school, her whole life ahead of her. Who would do such a thing?"

The elevator door opened on the third floor. Knowing the woman wasn't done talking, Gardy held the door open. He hoped she wouldn't keep him here too long. Gardy's Aunt Loraine could trap you at the doorway for hours on end, firing conversation starters when you touched the doorknob.

"Did you know Kacy Deering, ma'am?"

"No, I can't say I did, but in a village this small you know everyone's names."

Her eyes fell upon Gardy's ring finger and realized he was single. For goodness' sake, he thought. She's profiling me.

"You know..." Her lips curled into a grin, eyes full of life again as she fished through her purse. She produced a wallet-size photo of a pretty woman with flowing auburn curls. "My niece, Jenna."

Gardy shifted his feet.

"Isn't she pretty?"

"I...uh..."

"She's a real estate agent right here in Coral Lake. Oh, my. She's an agent, just like you."

Polite laughter.

"What a coincidence."

Get me the hell out of here.

"I should give you her number. Wait just a second, I know it's in here somewhere."

He could see room 301. Just a few steps away if he could escape the elevator. The woman rummaged through her pocketbook again. She really was his Aunt Loraine.

"It's not necessary, ma'am. I'll be leaving town soon."

The woman sighed.

"Look at me making a fool of myself, trying to play matchmaker. It's just that Jenna's so successful and pretty, but lousy with relationships just like my sister. Jenna's a good girl. She finally left that deadbeat husband of hers. The divorce hasn't gone through yet, but—"

"I really should go. Hey, it's such a beautiful afternoon. I bet you have a big day planned at the lake."

She beamed.

"Why, yes. I'm meeting Trish and Irena at the Bluefish Grill, then we're going on the boat cruise before Evelyn meets us at..."

"It was nice meeting you. And good luck to your niece."

He could still hear her talking as the elevator closed and the car began its painfully slow descent to the first floor.

Gardy raised his hand to knock on 301 and stopped. He took a breath and steeled himself, remembering the Walshes lives had turned upside-down.

A pretty black woman with long braids opened the door on the first knock.

"Lyra Walsh? I'm Special Agent Gardy."

"Yes, Mr. Gardy. We've been expecting you. Come in, please."

Gardy tried not to whistle. He figured a room like this ran five or six hundred a night as she led him inside. A sliding glass door took up most of the back wall and led out to a balcony, beyond which the lake sparkled and swelled. In the center of the room, a young boy sat on the floor with a parent's iPhone, tilting the phone and drumming his thumbs, lost inside a game.

"Nathan? The agent is here."

The bathroom sink shut off, and Nathan Walsh came into the main room towel drying his face. His skin was lighter than Lyra's, almost almond, hair cropped short. Nathan's gray slacks were designer, probably worth more than Gardy's entire wardrobe.

"Agent Gardy?"

Nathan shook his hand.

"Thank you for seeing me on short notice."

"Of course. Please have a seat."

Nathan sank into a cushioned armchair and pinched the bridge of his nose. Gardy sat across from him on the couch.

"My apologies for not answering the door," the man said. "I've been fighting a migraine since morning."

"Mr. Walsh, your family has been through a lot, and I don't want to take up all of your time."

"No need to apologize, Agent Gardy." He put his arm around Lyra, who stood by his side. "As you can see I have my whole family together, and for that I'm thankful."

Lyra pursed her lips.

"I wish we could say the same for the Deerings. Chase, why don't you play your game in the bedroom so we can talk."

Gardy watched the boy walk into the bedroom, shoulders slumped and feet dragging.

"I'm sorry, Mr. Gardy," Lyra said, waiting for the door to close. "This has been hard on all of us. Chase just wants to go home and have his bedroom back."

"I'm sure he does. Mr. Walsh, are you certain your son never heard anything?"

"Yes. Except for the upheaval, Chase is acting perfectly normal. He has no idea what happened."

"I see. How well did you know Kacy Deering?"

Nathan shared a look with his wife.

"We've known her for about two years. Is that right?"

Lyra nodded.

"We met Kacy through the United Methodist Church on Grant Street. Chase was three then." Lyra glanced at the bedroom door and ensured the boy wasn't eavesdropping. "She came recommended as a babysitter, and we'd used her ever since."

"Did she have any enemies?"

"I wouldn't know," Lyra said. "But then again she was a teenager, and sometimes kids develop rivalries."

"What about at church? Did you ever notice anyone pay too much attention to Kacy?"

"Not that I can recall."

Nathan rubbed the top of his head.

"We've been over all of this with the sheriff."

"I realize that, Mr. Walsh, but I want to be thorough. Finding out who did this is my only priority."

Lyra massaged Nathan's shoulders.

"Kacy was a nice girl. Dependable. And she was good with Chase."

"Kacy's boyfriend was inside your house Friday night. She brought alcohol."

Lyra glanced down at Nathan. His head tilted up and their eyes met.

"We suspected as much," Lyra said. "Kacy understood she wasn't to have friends over or drink when she babysat, but Nathan and I were teenagers once, too. She'd been with the Goodrich boy for a long time, at least since we moved to Coral Lake two years ago. You don't suspect he was...involved, do you?"

"We're looking into all possibilities."

"I can't imagine he'd do such a thing."

"What about friends and family? Does anyone have access to your house?"

Nathan moved Lyra's hands off his shoulders and rested his head against the chair.

"You mean extra keys?"

"Yes."

"The killer broke the front door window, Agent Gardy. He didn't need a key."

"I understand, but it's important we cover all bases."

Nathan exhaled.

"Yes, a few people have keys. For one, there's my brother, Kendall."

"Where is Kendall now?"

"Kalamazoo. He hasn't been to Coral Lake in over a year."

"Where can I reach your brother?"

Nathan rolled his eyes and opened his wallet. When he found his brother's business card, he handed it to Gardy, who copied the name and address and handed the card back.

"Thank you. Who else?"

"Well, there's Clyde Sullivan next door. He keeps an eye on the house when we go south for the winter."

It occurred to Gardy the Walshes were young to be snowbirds. Nathan recognized the question on Gardy's face.

"I consult for technology firms, mostly small startups, but I'm sure you've looked into my background already. I set my own hours and work from anywhere, a nice luxury when it's five below zero. Coral Lake might look like paradise, Agent Gardy, but check back in the middle of January."

"What about Chase? Doesn't he have school?"

"We home-school our son. It makes sense since we travel so often, and Lyra taught elementary school before my consulting work took off."

Gardy leaned forward on his knees and studied his shoes for a moment.

"I need to ask you something else, and I hope you won't take it the wrong way."

When he looked up Nathan was glaring at him.

"Then ask your question, Agent Gardy."

"Can you think of anyone who would want to hurt you or your family?"

"No, I cannot." Challenge filled his eyes. "Are you suggesting someone might hurt us because we are black?"

Gardy noticed Coral Lake was predominantly white, but nothing suggested racist undertones existed in the affluent town.

"Please, Mr. Walsh. That's not what I meant at all."

Lyra went back to rubbing the tension out of Nathan's shoulders. Nathan glared out the window.

"But it crossed your mind. Coral Lake has never been much for diversity, a blind man could see as much. And sure, the good townsfolk manage to misplace our invitations whenever the rich and famous hold their soirees. But this isn't 1960s Mississippi. We are as much a part of the community as anyone."

"I agree," Lyra said, moving to sit upon the armrest.

She held Nathan's hand. "Whoever perpetrated this vicious act, I can assure you he wasn't aiming for us."

CHAPTER SEVEN

The ashtray was a graveyard of shriveled cigarette butts. Stephanie Deering's kitchen sink overflowed with dishes, the counter dabbed by sauce and what appeared to be a chunk of fat. Sitting across from Bell at the kitchen table, Stephanie's hands trembled as she stacked a pile of spilled bills. She had Kacy's eyes and facial features, Bell thought. Time and a smoking addiction had parched and shriveled her skin, colored the tips of her fingers yellow. She wore a bathrobe over an old pair of sweatpants.

"They won't leave you alone, you know?"

Bell waved the smoke from her eyes and coughed into her hand as Deering fired up another cigarette. The tip glowed red and angry, then receded.

"Who won't leave you alone?"

"Creditors. Nothing but a bunch of vultures."

Bell knew from Lerner's briefing the father had left them two years ago and the Deerings had money problems.

"How often did Kacy's father contact her?"

Stephanie rolled her eyes.

"Christmas. Birthdays. That's about it. Couldn't be bothered the rest of the year."

"Is he still in Sacramento?"

"Far as I know. He wouldn't tell me if he moved, the son-of-a-bitch."

Bell glanced down at Lerner's notes.

"It says here you were working while Kacy babysat."

"Story of my life. Soon as I finish at the restaurant, I waitress at Marilyn's for another eight hours."

"Marilyn's. That's out on route 20, right?"

"That's right. About five miles out of town."

"How did Kacy get to the Walsh's?"

"She walked. It's only five-minutes away."

"Right, but afterward she'd have to walk in the dark."

Stephanie pounded the table. The stack of bills toppled over and spread out like the loser's hand in a game of poker. Fire flared in the woman's eyes.

"You think I wanted her walking home alone? You've seen that hill. Nothing but blind curves and no shoulder to speak of. I did what I could, Agent Bell." Stephanie picked up the bills and shook them. "Two jobs, and the rest of the time I cook and sleep. Someone had to pay the bills and save for college because you can bet her father wouldn't have helped."

A tear crawled out of her eye. She swiped it away.

"I'm sorry. None of this is your problem. I realize you're just trying to find who did this. Would you do that, agent? Would you find who hurt my girl?"

Bell reached across the table and touched her arm, a small gesture to let the woman know she sympathized.

"We'll find him, Mrs. Deering. I promise."

Stephanie sniffed and produced a ragged tissue. She stamped the cigarette out and slid the ashtray away.

"I'm sorry. It hits me at the strangest times, you know? Sometimes it's just the way the light moves across the kitchen, and I think it's time for Kacy to wake up and I'd better grab her before it gets too late. And then I remember."

Another tissue was in Stephanie's hands. She

sniffled.

Bell closed her notebook and put down the pen. It seemed to put Stephanie at ease.

"If you want to take a break—"

"No. Please continue. I want you to find who did this. I want you to find him and put a bullet in his head."

"I'll do everything I can to find him, Mrs. Deering. Let's talk about school."

"Sure."

"Did Kacy have enemies?"

"Not Kacy. Never. Don't get me wrong. She wasn't one of the popular girls, but she never had a problem with any of them."

"No fights, no drama?"

"Nothing like that. I don't think the in-crowd knew she existed."

Bell could relate. She'd floated through high school like a ghost, clinging to a tight-knit group of friends, barely acknowledged by the various cliques.

"What about boys?"

Stephanie smiled wistfully, eyes turning misty again.

"She was…is…a very pretty girl, my Kacy. Lots of boys were interested. Not that I was home much, but when I was the phone rang off the hook, always some boy looking for her."

Bell sat forward and held Stephanie's eyes.

"Did any boy pay your daughter an unusual amount of attention, perhaps too much?"

"Well, she was with Braden. Lots of boys tried and tried, but she was happy dating Braden."

Stephanie's brow wrinkled. She paused, lips moving as if working out a problem in her head.

"Mrs. Deering?"

"Now that you mention it there was one boy who took things too far."

Grabbing the pen, Bell reopened the notebook.

"What was the boy's name?"

"Ethan, I think." Stephanie nodded. "Yes, Ethan Lancaster."

"When you say he took things too far, what exactly do you mean?"

"Let me think for a moment. This was two years ago when Kacy was only a sophomore. He was an older boy, a senior, but he'd failed a grade way back. He used to call Kacy several times a day. Likely more than that, because sometimes I'd pick up the phone and there'd just be silence on the other end."

"Did Kacy ever tell him to stop?"

"At first, I think she was flattered. The idea of an older boy and all, and this was before she dated Braden. But the calls kept coming, and that worried Kacy. And me, of course. He wouldn't take no for an answer."

Hurriedly scribbling notes, Bell glanced up.

"Mrs. Deering, at any point did Kacy think someone was following her?"

"Ethan broke into her bedroom one night."

Bell froze.

"Broke in? Did he hurt Kacy?"

"No. I caught him before he...I don't want to think about what he intended."

"Your daughter's room is on the second floor. How did he get up that high?"

"There's a lattice running up the back of the house," Stephanie said, pushing up from her chair. Bell followed her across the kitchen where they peered along the backside of the little two-story. A vining plant, dead and wilted, snaked through the lattice. "See what I mean?"

"I see it. I hardly think it would support my weight. How big was Ethan?"

"Bigger than you. Heavier, too. What you do is climb a

few feet and stand on the window sill. Otherwise, the lattice will snap. From there you grab the lower roof and pull yourself up if you have strong arms. Or if you're light like me."

Craning her neck, Bell looked up the side of the house. The climb appeared awfully steep.

"Sounds like you've done this before."

"Agent Bell, I'm coming and going so often I can't count the number of times I've locked myself out of the house."

Bell wanted to get a better look at the lattice and window from the backyard. She filed a mental note to do so when the interview finished. They returned to the table. Stephanie slumped into her chair.

"Back to Ethan. Did he break the window?"

"No. It was summer and Kacy left her window open, which I told her not to do on account of the weatherman calling for storms. Still, he needed to pop the screen out of the window. That's how I heard him."

"Please tell me you called the sheriff."

"Wasn't anything they could do. It was dark, and I never got a good look at his face. Besides, if you think Sheriff Lerner is a waste of space, you should have known Sheriff Myers. What a piece of work."

"Did they question Ethan?"

"Oh, sure. They sent a deputy to the Lancaster's house. The boy claimed he was in bed sick that night, and the father vouched for him. You can always tell a Lancaster is lying when their lips move."

After the interview finished, Bell photographed the lattice and searched for additional entry points. In the hot interior of the rental car, Bell sat in silence. The wind ran up and over the windshield and made a whistling noise. She recalled no mention of Ethan Lancaster in Lerner's briefing, which struck her as odd.

Bell turned the key and rolled down the windows when the engine fired. Her clothes smelled like an ashtray and she wanted a shower.

Before she took the car out of gear, she dialed Gardy. The special agent was just leaving the Coral Lake Suites when he answered.

"We have a problem, Gardy."

"Yeah?"

"Kacy had a stalker."

CHAPTER EIGHT

Gardy was waiting in the village common with Sheriff Lerner when Bell pulled the car curbside. The shoppers strolling the sidewalk all stared at her. They knew who she was, and it reminded them of the danger hiding within the village.

Lerner, who'd carried a dejected disposition from the moment he met them at the airport, suddenly beamed.

"Yeah, I know all about Ethan Lancaster. He worked with Norwood Construction until recently before the guy up and broke the foreman's nose over some petty bullshit. Ethan is a hothead and a violent one at that. About a week afterward we nailed him on a DUI. It's one thing after another with that guy. I've been saying it's only a matter of time before he does something crazy, but I never expected anything like this."

"Slow down," Gardy said. "It's a helluva leap to go from bar fights and climbing through a girl's window to hacking her into pieces."

"Is it a leap? I thought that's how these serial killers get started. Committing sex crimes and the like."

Bell shook the windblown hair from her eyes and lowered her voice as a middle-aged couple passed.

"Except he didn't rape her."

"Well, I might not know much about profiling, but I guarantee you Ethan Lancaster did this."

The sheriff's office was a brick building with white columns running up the front. By the time they arrived, Deputy Crandall, a young and muscular man with short stubble popping out of his face, said Ethan Lancaster was already on his way.

The tiny office was cramped with desks, making it a challenge to weave toward the back. The interrogation room was gloomy and held a small table with two plastic chairs on the left end and one on the right.

Ethan took longer to arrive than expected. A half-hour later Deputy Crandall led Ethan into the room. The man sat across from Bell and Gardy, rocking back on his chair and chewing on a wad of gum. There was a chip missing from a front tooth, otherwise Bell thought women might have found Ethan attractive. The beginnings of a beard circled his round face, hair tied on top of his head. A man bun, she laughed to herself. What kind of bad boy sports a man bun? The younger man looked strong, physique thick and pudgy, muscles crafted from hard labor rather than a gym membership. Physically he fit the rough profile she'd shaped in her head. The human body was built to survive trauma. Bones were hard, muscle tendons tough and resilient. It took strength to chop a body into pieces.

The deputy waited for Gardy's signal, then stepped outside the door.

Gardy nodded at Bell to begin.

"Thank you for coming in, Ethan. I'm Agent Bell, and this is Agent Gardy."

She reached across the table to shake his hand. He glanced at it and kept rocking back, a derisive grin on his face. Bell pulled her hand back and flipped open Ethan's folder.

"You're a busy man. In the last year alone, an assault,

a DUI, and two separate charges for public intoxication."

He leered.

"The assault was bullshit. Guy swung on me first."

She shuffled through the papers, shaking her head in wonder. It seemed Ethan couldn't stay out of trouble.

"Tell me more about the assault."

"It was a fight."

"Okay, the fight."

Ethan rocked forward. The metal chair legs clonked down on the floor.

"Gerry gave me shit about not working an extra hour. We were falling behind on a roofing job, which was his fault for taking on too many jobs in the first place. Told him I was busy, that I had shit to do and couldn't stay. Gerry said either I worked the extra hour and finished the job or he'd fire me, so I told him I'd sue his ass. You can't force someone to work extra hours without paying them. I mean, this is America. Right?"

"Then what happened?"

"Gerry got up in my face and acted tough, said he'd throw my ass off the site himself if I ever talked to him like that again. I told him to try. By then the rest of the guys had come over to watch the shit-show. Guess Gerry felt he needed to prove his manhood now that we had an audience. He shoved me, I shoved him. You know how it goes. I guess it got a little out of hand with the both of us screaming. I don't even remember hitting him. I mean, one minute he's yelling in my face, and the next he's on his back, nose all crooked and bleeding, and I got two guys on my arms pulling me away."

"You said he hit you first," said Gardy, sharing a glance with Bell.

"If I said that's what happened, then that's what happened."

"Ethan," Bell said, resting her elbows on the table and

propping her chin up with her hands. "Is it common for you to hit someone and not remember?"

Ethan's eyes darted between Bell and Gardy.

"I get mad sometimes is all."

"So it's possible you've hurt someone in the past and don't even remember doing it."

Ethan's fingers curled and uncurled in his lap, clenching into fists, knuckles white.

"I see what you're doing. Trying to put words in my mouth. If this is about that bitch, you can forget it."

"What bitch?"

Ethan was almost shouting now. He rose a few inches off the chair and leaned aggressively across the table.

"Kacy Deering. Who else would we be talking about? I mean, that's why I'm here, right? Because you think I was the one who did it."

The door opened. Deputy Crandall met Gardy's eyes, and the special agent raised a hand to say the situation was under control. Crandall nodded and returned to his post, glaring at Ethan until the door closed.

"Two years ago you broke into Kacy's bedroom."

"You can't prove that."

"Are you denying it happened? The mother says she saw your face."

Bell didn't blink over the lie. For the first time since the interview began, Ethan looked visibly rattled. Not surprising as for two years he'd believed it was too dark for Stephanie Deering to see.

"You got it all wrong."

"Good. That's why we're here, Ethan. Not to accuse anyone, but to clear up misconceptions and set the record straight." She flipped to a blank page and clicked her pen. "Why don't you tell us what really happened?"

The tension fell out of Ethan's shoulders. He seemed to shrink several inches as he slouched down in the chair.

"First of all, I didn't break into Kacy's bedroom. She invited me."

"Were you and Kacy lovers?"

"I wasn't dating her if that's what you mean. Look, it wasn't any secret that Kacy liked to play around. And when she did, she liked it dangerous."

Gardy glanced sidelong at Bell and led with the next question.

"How do you mean?"

"Like sneaking guys into her room when her mother was down the hall."

"You say you didn't break into the room, but the mother heard you knock the screen out of its tracks."

Ethan squinted up at the ceiling for a moment, then vigorously shook his head.

"No, no, no. Definitely not what happened. Kacy lifted the screen and let me inside. The thing is it was dark, and her nightstand was right up against the window. I kicked over a picture frame before my eyes adjusted."

"Then what?"

Ethan smirked.

"Use your imagination."

"I don't have much of an imagination, Ethan, so I prefer you humor me."

Sitting back and stretching out his legs, Ethan locked his fingers behind his head.

"We got in bed."

"Did you have sexual intercourse with Kacy Deering?"

"We would have. She was into it, and it got pretty hot in there. That's when we heard her mother running down the hall. Now, I figured Kacy was gonna tell me to hide. Maybe under the bed or such. But the bitch screams rape, for Christ's sake. I swear that's how it went down."

"You didn't force yourself on Kacy?"

"I'm not bragging, Agent Gardy, but I don't need to

rape a girl to get action. I damn near broke my neck climbing out that window in the dark. I had to swing from the lattice over to the porch roof, and I almost lost it trying to slide down the rail. Then I'm running through the yard and staying in the shadows, and all this time I can hear her whore mother screaming she's gonna call the cops."

The room was quiet for a moment. The fluorescent lights buzzed and flickered. Bell watched Ethan fidget, a clue he might not be telling the whole truth.

"That must have made you angry as hell," Bell said. "Kacy throwing you under the bus like that."

Ethan paused, measuring carefully what he said next.

"I wasn't happy but I moved on. Lots of fish in the sea, as the saying goes."

"That seems a little hard to believe. If you'll indulge me for a moment…" Bell flipped through the notes from Stephanie Deering's interview. "The mother remembers you called Kacy several times a day."

More squirming.

"I take it you have a problem hearing the word 'no.'"

The young man worked his jaw back-and-forth. They could hear his teeth grind.

"The only problem I have is putting up with bullshit lies. Like Kacy pretending she didn't invite me into her room. Bitch only did it to save her ass. Yeah, maybe I called her a few times."

"Maybe more than a few times?"

"You got proof of that?"

"Where were you Friday night?"

A wolfish grin formed on Ethan's face. It showed too many teeth.

"Drinking beer with my old man."

"Out in public where someone saw you?"

"Nah, just at his place. Thirty-two Pleasant Street, about half-a-mile from here as the crow flies. Now that's a silly saying, isn't it? As the crow flies. Makes you wonder who starts this shit."

Gardy picked up his phone.

"If I were to call your father now…"

"Yeah, he'd vouch for me. Bet that puts a serious crank in your shorts, me having an alibi and all."

After Ethan left, Sheriff Lerner made a call to Corey Lancaster. He leaned against his desk, arms folded. Bell and Gardy sat across from him as the final vestiges of daylight burned at the window.

"His story checks out. Corey Lancaster claims his son was with him Friday night until two in the morning. Of course, the apple doesn't fall far from the tree. The father might be lying."

Bell didn't think so. To the sheriff's consternation, she ruled out Ethan as the murderer. Besides, Braden Goodrich had arrived.

Though she knew Kacy's boyfriend didn't fit the profile, they went through with the interview. The boy was visibly distraught and cried repeatedly, blaming himself for not staying with Kacy.

"I was gonna go back and drive her home," he said, wiping his eyes on the collar of his shirt. "I figured I'd drive around for a little bit and wait for her up the road."

"Did you call Kacy?"

"No…no, I didn't."

She already knew he hadn't called but wanted to confirm the boy was being honest. The phone history showed no calls from Braden that evening.

"But you worried over Kacy walking home in the dark. Why didn't you call?"

He dropped his eyes. Shrugged once and shook his head.

"Because I was mad."

"You were upset with Kacy?"

"It's stupid, okay? I thought she wanted…I mean…"

"You thought she wanted to have sex with you."

"Well, yeah."

"And you became angry when she didn't want to."

He shifted in his seat, looked off into a shadowed corner.

"I wasn't angry. Just hurt." He choked on his words and fell silent. "I can't believe she's gone."

Bell ran through the rest of her questions. She knew full well Braden Goodrich had nothing to do with Kacy's murder.

On their way back to the hotel, Gardy and Bell ate fish sandwiches on the pier. Dusk settled over the village and slashed streaks of magenta across the blue lake waters. The last tour boat of the evening left port. Shop owners turned off the lights and locked doors.

"You feel that?"

Gardy looked at her, confused.

"It's fear," she said, continuing.

The setting sun took the villagers' resolve with it, dragging it into the ground. The few people remaining on the street hustled to their cars with lowered heads and hands cupping arms, wearily glancing up now-and-then as if expecting someone to leap out of the shadows.

"Makes you wonder if the village will ever be the same."

Gardy sighed.

"We both know that answer. Before Friday, nobody could conceive something this horrible was possible. Maybe in New York City or Rochester or Buffalo. Not in Coral Lake."

The breeze off the water was chilling. It would take another month before the cold breath of winter disappeared from its depths. Bell rubbed goosebumps off her arms.

"Maybe we should go someplace warmer."

They found a bench in the village park. Cut in silhouette, a mother duck led a train of ducklings across the water. The tour boat was nothing but a blinking light on the horizon.

"So it doesn't appear Ethan Lancaster is our guy," Gardy said, watching the boat vanish. "That is if we believe the father."

"He doesn't fit the profile, regardless."

"No, he doesn't."

"Our guy is a loner. He might go out for a drink, but I guarantee he sits at the end of the bar away from everyone else. I don't see him holding an office job. Too many people would look at him. So if he happens to work in an office, he has a corner cubicle."

Gardy stuck his hands into his pockets and jiggled his legs to stay warm.

"You believe he watched Kacy for a long time, months perhaps. So I agree."

"He was likely abused as a child. No siblings and a one-parent household. The unknown subject needed space to hide and construct his own fantasies of dominating and controlling others."

"That ties back to why he stole Kacy's clothes."

"And scalping her, though that was rather unexpected."

"What do you think that represents?"

"I don't think the clothes and hair are necessarily trophies, at least not in the way these guys usually think. No, I feel he's keeping her alive. For himself. And that tells me she was special to him."

At the clicking of heels, Bell lowered her voice as a woman strode along the sidewalk.

"Somehow he knew her."

"In a village this small it's not hard to believe," said Gardy. "But that doesn't explain how she was special to him.

A neighbor, perhaps?"

Keys jingled with desperate intensity as the woman looked over her shoulder. Her eyes locked on Gardy's and Bell's shadows, then she whipped open the car door and drove off without turning on her headlights.

"Yes, possibly a neighbor. Except Lerner interviewed the Deering's neighbors and nobody fit the profile. Loner, strong."

"Then not a neighbor. He saw her in a different setting. We could go round and round for hours and never get close to an answer. Look around. In daylight, I could sit on this bench and watch a hundred girls walk through the park."

"Right," she snickered. "And ask them if they were a Pisces."

"I'm just saying. If you were really obsessed with someone, you wouldn't have to go far to watch them every day in this village. It's supposed to hit 80 degrees by Saturday. I bet half the town will be in the park."

Bell leaned forward, elbows on knees.

"We missed something at the Walsh house."

"Between the crime scene techs, deputies, and our walk-through, I think we covered all the bases."

Bell rubbed at her temples and closed her eyes.

"No. Something isn't right about the break-in. I want to look again."

"Okay, but it can wait until tomorrow. It won't do us any good to paw around in the dark."

No, she thought. It can't wait until tomorrow. I need to figure out what I missed.

In the end, she decided he was right.

But time had already run out for them.

CHAPTER NINE

Angela Thiele hated this part of her job. The employee parking spaces stood at the back of the lot, away from the lamps and the pharmacy's brightness.

The paper bag was in her hand, filled with blood pressure medication for Mrs. Ives. It crinkled and brushed her legs as she walked, her shoes clonking against the blacktop. She could see her father's Nissan Rogue under a clump of trees, the vehicle's white glow barely visible, and she chided herself for parking in the shadows during the heat of the day so the sun wouldn't bake the interior. What difference would it make? Her deliveries didn't begin until after dark, and closing time was midnight. Now the mosquitoes nipped at her, the air uncomfortably cool without a jacket.

The shifting wind brought music from the village square as she passed between two cars. She had to turn sideways to squeeze through, the bag of medicine held above her head as she danced between the parked vehicles. It felt strange that nobody was in the parking lot except her. No customers. No employees taking a smoke break. Scary, like strolling through a graveyard at midnight.

The parking lot opened to a vast, desert-like empty space. It was ridiculous Mr. Ripple made the employees park this far from the store. The lot was never more than quarter-full during peak hours. What would be the harm in allowing her to park near the lamp lights? She would be sure to bring it up to him before she left for school in August. If he became angry, it would be no skin off her back. This was just a summer job. Next year she'd be sure to apply at the marina. Anywhere but the pharmacy.

The keys jangled in Angela's hand as she approached the Rogue. She needed to weave between Karla's Jeep and Ron's Volkswagen to reach her father's vehicle. Close now. Only a few more seconds alone in the dark.

She saw the van parked beside the Rogue. It was too close. The sides brushed up against her driver side door. Her first worry—how would she explain it to her father if the van scratched the exterior? Then her worry turned to irritation. Even if the Rogue was unscathed, she'd have a helluva time squeezing into the driver's seat. She might need to crawl in through the passenger side and shimmy over the gearshift. If she ripped her skirt doing so, she'd take her keys and rip a long, sharp line down the side of the shitty van. Whose van was it, anyway? It wasn't Ripple's. Angela didn't know what kind of vehicle he drove, but she bet her life he eschewed the employee parking rules and pulled up close to the pharmacy.

When she reached the Rogue's bumper she peered down the tunnel formed by the van and her father's vehicle. It was a tight squeeze for sure, but she thought there was just enough room to wiggle through and pry open the door. If her door clipped the side of the van, tough shit. That's what you get for parking too close.

She edged sideways past the van and took in its shabby appearance. Rust pockmarked the sides. The bulk leaned slightly to the right, something wrong with the undercarriage or whatever held vehicles upright. She didn't know much about how vehicles were built and didn't particularly care as long as they got her where she needed to go.

Halfway to her door, she noticed a long, metal box through the van's windows. It was probably filled with tools, yet its presence made her skin prickle. It looked too much like a casket.

The way forward constricted. The van was angled slightly to the right. Too tight. But the door was so close she could reach out and touch it with the tips of her fingers.

Stubbornly, she pushed forward. And stopped.

The van trapped her against the Rogue, pressing against her skirted thighs. A nervous giggle and Angela reversed course, admitting defeat. This wasn't such a good idea. Better to try the passenger door.

Except she couldn't move.

The ridiculous predicament might have made her laugh had she not been alone in the dark, the pharmacy on the other side of the lot seeming a million miles away. Panic rose in her throat. She thought of calling for help but didn't want the indignation of someone finding her in this predicament. No, she could get herself out of this. She needed to stay calm and think things through.

Angela stepped sideways. The rusty van scraped at her thigh and seemed to bite down. The girl yelped and shoved her hands against the van's bulk, hoping she could force her way backward and buy herself a fraction of wiggle room. When that failed, she gripped the top of the van and struggled to pull herself up. Her legs writhed between the vehicles, their cold exteriors like dead hands against her flesh. Struggling only worsened her situation. The two vehicles crunched the bulge of one kneecap, the pain excruciating. She yelped and twisted toward the back door until her body popped free.

She bent over to touch the throbbing knee and froze. She wasn't alone in the parking lot.

As she clutched the keys and limped out from between the vehicles, the man's silhouette filled the tunnel.

Before she could react, the pipe wrench came down on her head.

The night spun. She crumpled to the pavement. Fingers brushed against her father's Rogue as a powerful hand gripped under her arms and dragged.

To the van. Eyes fluttered as unconsciousness pulled her down and down.

The door slid open.

And then there was only darkness.

CHAPTER TEN

The alarm tore Bell out of a dream. She glanced at the window, through which morning light shone brightly. Rubbing the sleep out of her eyes, she checked her phone and found two missed calls from Gardy and a message.

Where the heck are you? Call me.

Her hands were jittery as she rolled through her phone settings. Bell's mother used to tell her she could sleep through a tornado, but lately the slightest noise awakened her and often left her anxious and unable to close her eyes for the rest of the night. The settings confirmed the ringer was off. She certainly hadn't turned the phone off. Damn Apple.

She started texting Gardy when he knocked on the door. Throwing the sheets back, she climbed from the bed and rushed to the door. The mirror stopped her as she touched the lock. She wasn't dressed to answer the door. The nightshirt barely made it past her hips.

"Bell, you okay?"

Her answer came out as a croak. She cleared her throat.

"Just a second."

She pulled on a pair of sweatpants and brushed her fingers through the rat's nest atop her head. Not exactly presentable, but it would have to do.

When she pulled open the door his eyes were averted toward something interesting on the rug. Clearly he expected her to be less than decent.

"It's okay. Come in."

Gardy cautiously rolled his eyes back to the doorway until he verified she was clothed. He raised his hands as if to say, *why in the hell won't you answer your phone?*

"I know, I know. My ringer was off. Don't ask me how." She sat on the edge of the bed, the sheets and blankets a rumpled mess. "What's going on?"

"Our target might have struck again last night."

"Oh, Jesus. Where was the body?"

"No, there isn't a body. Not yet anyway. Let's hope it's just a coincidence, but I have my doubts."

She chewed a nail as he sat on the ottoman, elbows on knees, looking down. He rarely met her eyes when he was nervous.

"Then I take it we have a missing person."

"Another teenage girl. The sheriff's office took a call about an hour ago from the parents of Angela Thiele. She hasn't been seen since halfway through her shift at Brockhart's Pharmacy yesterday evening, and she was due to get off work at midnight."

"Wait. The parents are just reporting this now? What took so long?"

"Apparently she sleeps in late after work, not too different from some people I know." He shot her a meaningful glare. "So nobody thought twice when she didn't come down for breakfast. The father was the first to notice his Nissan Rogue wasn't in the driveway when he went outside to grab the garbage cans. Even then they figured she'd spent the night at a girlfriend's house."

Bell was up now and digging through her bag for something to wear.

"What time did the pharmacy say she left?"

"Lerner pulled the manager out of bed an hour ago. Guy named Derrick Ripple. He said Thiele went out for a delivery run around nine o'clock and that was the last he saw of her. Apparently he'd overheard the girl telling a coworker she was thinking about quitting, so Ripple figured she'd blown off the delivery."

"Idiot."

"Lerner said as much about the guy. Regardless, the sheriff's department found the Rogue at the back of the lot where the employees are supposed to park. The side door is all scuffed up, maybe a sign of a struggle. They're testing for DNA now."

Bell grabbed a change of clothes and headed for the bathroom, leaving the door half-open so they could continue speaking.

"You think it's the same guy? Kacy's killer, I mean?"

Gardy exhaled.

"If it's the same guy, he struck awfully fast again. That in itself is unusual. It's a different pattern, too."

She spat toothpaste and leaned her head through the doorway.

"Maybe not a new pattern at all. Perhaps he thought the lot was too risky to kill the girl, so he needed to take her somewhere."

"Which is why we have to figure out where he took her…if this is our guy."

Bell didn't need to reply. It was the same person who killed Kacy Deering. Gardy knew it, too.

A half-hour later they were inside the sheriff's office. The parents were there. Bell estimated they were both around forty-five-years-old. The father had a thick mat of black hair and wore a golf shirt and khakis. The mother's clothes suggested she was ready to work in the garden before the panic began. She leaned her head against her husband's shoulder, eyes flashing around the room like birds trapped in a greenhouse. After they interviewed the parents, Gardy and Bell sat in chairs across from Lerner. The sheriff sat behind his desk. Bell caught the hint of a quiver when Lerner moved his hands, the sheriff obviously overwhelmed.

Lerner removed his hat and rubbed at his forehead.

"What do we do now?"

"We keep rattling the bushes," Gardy said. "Brockhart's is close to the village square, isn't it?"

"About a block-and-a-half away."

"Then chances are somebody saw the guy's vehicle. Call in anyone off work today and canvas the neighborhood. Talk to Angela's coworkers. Ask if anyone saw an unusual vehicle hanging around the lot, something that didn't fit."

Bell tapped the pen against her cheek, thinking.

"In particular, focus on vans seen in the area. See if that rings a bell with anyone. We're dealing with an abduction now, and while it's not impossible the unknown subject drives a car, he likely used a van."

Lerner blinked.

"That makes sense. Would be easier to catch the girl and throw her inside."

"Not only that, but it gives him a greater sense of isolation and solitude, and I believe that's very important to him. In the meantime, hold the Thieles a little longer and get Stephanie Deering to come in. There has to be a common relation between them, someone who knew Kacy and Angela."

Lerner slapped his hands on his desk.

"I'll call Crandall and get him in early."

When they were out of earshot Bell leaned close to Gardy.

"I still want to look at the Walsh house."

"You sure? The priority is finding the link between Kacy and Angela. You said so, yourself."

"I missed something important, Gardy. The sooner I figure out what it is, the better. It's our best chance to find Angela."

"First we need to check out the area around the pharmacy. Talk to people. This will take most of the day."

"I understand. When we have a moment."

With a shared glance, she and Gardy agreed to revisit the Walsh house after they exhausted their remaining options.

Bell noticed the Thieles staring. She nodded back at them, a promise to do her best and bring their child home alive. They dropped their eyes to the floor.

CHAPTER ELEVEN

The bare bulb casts harsh light inside the tight confines of the shed. When Hodge moves the shadows are elongated, grotesque. It makes him edgy, makes him clutch his hair and yank. His hands come away with a clump which he brushes on his jeans.

Inside the shed, the heat builds, humidity bleeding rivulets of sweat down his neck, soaking his shirt and producing a greasy vinegar stench. The sun will soon set judging by the long shadows cutting among the trees. It will be warm tonight. The full heat of summer has arrived in Coral Lake. Winter no longer sleeps in the shadows. He should shower, he thinks. He should clean himself so he is presentable to the women. It is true they are under his control, but decency is important. The problem is the shower is in his home inside the village, and he can't leave them alone.

The girl is asleep on the cot. Her wrists are bound behind her back by rope, knees drawn to her stomach. When she breathes her chest swells and recedes, a gentle lake tide he wishes to touch and swim within. There will be time for that. They have the rest of their lives together.

Sharing the cot is Kacy, the girl he continues to hide from Mother.

He isn't insane, Hodge tells himself, understanding the mannequin isn't flesh and bone. When he runs his nailed fingers over the mannequin's skin, it is stiff and cool to the touch. Dressed in Kacy's clothes, the pelt fixed upon its head, the life-size doll *is* Kacy. Squinting, he observes her chest and wills the flesh to expand and contract as does the other girl's.

He reaches out, desires to touch the new girl's skin. She has slept a long time. Occasionally the girl mutters and squirms, legs running dog-like in her sleep. Apprehension grips him. The new girl will love him as Kacy does. Yet she is deep in a dream now and will be frightened by the sudden touch.

Her skin is tan and young and perfect. He can no longer help himself.

Hands poised over her breast. A trickle of spittle crawling from the corner of his mouth.

A scream comes out of the forest. He backs away. Eyes move between Kacy and the sleeping girl. If they hear, neither reacts. They continue to sleep side-by-side. Sisters. No, more than sisters. They share a bond linked inextricably to him.

Still no reaction from the girls.

Careful not to wake them, he shuffles to the entryway. Cracks the door open and squints. Though the day grows long, the outside world is brighter than the shed. He can see the van beyond a stand of trees. The small clearing in which the shed resides is vacant. Overgrown grass ripples in the wind.

Hodge begins to shut the door when the shrill voice rings out again. Shouting his name.

Eyes lock on the van. Silently, he pleads for her to be quiet before she draws attention. But she won't stop. Keeps yelling his name, voice warbling on the edge of hoarseness.

He closes the door and stands with his back pressed against the frame. Breaths heave in-and-out as he watches them sleep. Mother's yells are frenzied and grow in volume until he is sure his ears will bleed. Cannot understand why the girls haven't awakened.

Finally it is too much for him to handle, and he throws open the door. The shed rattles with his fury. Heedless of the girls, he slams the door shut and stalks toward the van. Hands clutch ears and try to smother the infernal screams.

He comes upon the van and yanks on the sliding door. Meets resistance as Mother's yells echo inside. Locked. He'd forgotten it was locked.

Head darting around the forest, he fishes the keys from his pocket. Inserts the key into the locking mechanism and twists. An empty popping sound.

Hodge wrenches the door open and climbs inside. He is enraged by her, yet confused. He gave her the gift of perpetual, immutable sleep, and she will not sleep, will not be quiet or allow him to live in peace.

From his back pocket, he removes the knife. Touches the edge to his thumb and draws blood.

He will teach Mother to be silent again. To obey.

The trunk rattles and bucks, shaking the van. She knows what he intends.

She screams his name, tries to intimidate and recapture dominance over him. He is evolved and beyond her.

He fumbles with the locks and throws the trunk open.

CHAPTER TWELVE

Something shook the cot. A loud thump.

Angela's eyes opened to the dingy shed. Her vision was blurry, eyelids crusted shut by sleep and tears. She didn't know where she was and became confused by the cramped confines. Around her rose the thick, hot scent of baked wood.

Then she recalled the nighttime walk through the parking lot. The shadowed man blocking her escape route.

Remembering him striking her with the wrench brought pain. Angela's head throbbed and turned her thoughts cloudy.

She'd recognized the man. What was his name? Hodge. Her parents hired him to install insulation in the basement. She didn't know much about home repair, but she found it curious that the job dragged out for multiple days, Hodge always finding some new problem which required him to return. She didn't like being alone in the house with him. The way he leered at her from the corner of his eye. He didn't think she noticed, but a girl senses eyes on her.

The memory of the abduction pulled her up from sleep's depths into a new nightmare. She twisted on the filthy mattress. Rope cut into her wrists.

Someone shouted. She couldn't tell where it came from. The way it echoed told her she was somewhere outside, perhaps in the wilderness.

Angela struggled to turn herself over and heard yelling again. She was about to scream for help when the truth came to her. The voice belonged to Hodge. Who was he yelling at?

She wiggled her wrists and fought to pull her hands through the bindings. Sweat poured down her arms and made the rope slick. This was good, she thought. It might be enough to free her hands.

Yet he'd bound her good. The fight hurt Angela and made it feel as though she might dislocate her wrists.

When she turned over, the mannequin face stared back at her with dead eyes. She cried out. Swallowing the next scream and praying Hodge hadn't heard, she wiggled backward to the edge of the cot, away from the glaring monstrosity. To Angela's horror, the mannequin wore a teen girl's clothing—a halter top and cut-off jean shorts with manufactured rips down the thighs. Affixed to its head was a pelt of dark hair. A wig, she thought, until she noticed the smear of dried blood along the doll's scalp. She almost screamed again as her tears flowed.

Angela swung her legs into the air and used momentum to sit up. She couldn't peel her eyes away from the mannequin-thing. It seemed to watch her, inviting her to stay here forever, wherever here was. It struck her the clothes and hair must be Kacy Deering's, and then there was nothing she could do to prevent herself from crying out, delirious. She dropped forward and buried her mouth against the dirty bed. Let it suffocate her screams until she couldn't cry anymore.

Her shoulders shook as she pulled herself into a sitting position. She struggled to compose her thoughts and buried the roiling panic trying to confuse her. Angela twisted her head so she couldn't see the mannequin-thing anymore, but she felt its eyes on her back as she stood up. Her legs buckled.

The wall saved her. She slumped against the side of the shed until feeling returned to her legs. Looking down, she saw scraped flesh across her thighs and purplish bruising on her kneecaps.

It was quiet outside the shed. She couldn't hear Hodge anymore.

Which meant whoever he was yelling at might have disabled him.

Or he'd heard Angela and was coming back to the shed.

The door latch was low to the ground. Angela needed to bend at the knees and squat, facing away from the door. She groped behind her for the latch and cursed the ropes, then found the mechanism with her fingers. Pulled up and found it locked. This couldn't be. It had to be unlocked. She wasn't meant to die here. She pushed down until the latch screeched and popped. Quietly, she wedged her fingers between the door and frame and inched it open. Nobody was coming.

The sun was almost down when she shuffled through the entryway. She heard birds and tasted the sweet freshness of natural air.

Her legs almost failed her as she stepped outside. Then she found her footing and moved faster with no idea where she was or where she was going. Everything looked the same around the clearing. Trees and overgrowth. Taloned shadows reaching toward her, growing as the light faded.

She walked faster, cutting between trees until she found the van. She froze in place. The side door was thrown open, but she didn't see Hodge. Careful of where she stepped, she slipped through the forest, cutting away from the van. Even if he'd left the keys in the ignition, she couldn't drive with her hands tied behind her back. She still didn't know where she was when it occurred to her the van must be on some sort of driveway or path. And that meant a road must be near.

Crouching down, she peered toward the van until she noticed the worn track leading down an incline. She climbed over a stump and spotted the road at the bottom of the hill. Below the road, amid the relics of daylight, Coral Lake shimmered in the valley bowl. She knew where she was now. Civilization was close.

Angela was past the van and struggling through the forest when she heard him coming. He screamed with insanity, berating Angela for leaving him, yelling something about betrayal. She didn't dare look behind. He was close. She heard him stomp through the overgrowth.

She broke out of the forest and cried for help as the earth swallowed the sun, and darkness dripped from the sky.

Hodge smashed through the trees. Right behind her.

CHAPTER THIRTEEN

"What the hell were you thinking?"

Bell brought her fist down on the hood of Sheriff Lerner's truck. Lerner jumped and stammered.

"Please try to understand. Nathan and Lyra Walsh just want to put their lives back together."

"They're staying at a boutique resort through the weekend. They could have waited another day. What was the rush?"

Gardy stepped between them and placed his hands on Bell's shoulders. Their eyes locked, Bell's bloodshot and burning with fury.

"There's nothing we can do about it now," said Gardy. "No reason we can't do another walk-through, make sure we covered all the bases."

She bulled past Gardy. The sheriff took a step backward and bumped into the Ram's door.

"Please," Lerner said, hands raised, trying to mollify the special agent before she bit his head off. "Try to see things from their perspective. It's just a piece of glass."

He gestured at the new pane in the door. Bell slapped her palm against her forehead.

"It's a crucial piece of evidence."

She took another step forward, and Lerner slid along the side of the truck until he leaned back over the cab.

"Now, calm down. There's a perfectly good reason for fixing the door. The weatherman is calling for storms overnight, and the Walshes can't exactly have rain pouring through a missing pane."

Again Gardy moved to intervene, this time clutching Bell's arms and walking her away from the sheriff.

"Get off me, Gardy!"

"Then get yourself under control."

"I'm perfectly under control."

She looked over her shoulder at the entryway, saw a fireball of setting sun reflecting in the glass. That's when it clicked.

Bell tugged free of her partner's grip and stomped up the steps. The new glass, shimmering and perfect, not a hint of dust or a child's fingerprints, stood out from the others. Even so, she swung around and pointed at the repaired pane.

"Is this the piece?"

"Yes," Lerner said, cautiously shuffling into the yard. "As I said, it's no big deal—"

Pulling the sleeve of her jacket over her hand, Bell whacked the pane with the outside of her fist. The new pane shattered and tinkled down in the foyer.

"What…I can't believe…Agent Gardy, do something before she wrecks the house."

Gardy scowled as he crossed the yard, his shoes making swishing noises through the grass.

"She's not gonna wreck the house." When he clonked up the stairs to Bell's side, he raised his eyebrows. "You aren't gonna wreck the house, right?"

It was clear to Bell Gardy was trying to diffuse the situation with humor. The glint in her partner's eyes told her he was on the same page. Behind them, Lerner paced back-and-forth. His hands clawed at his face while he muttered about lunatic agents and how he would explain this to the Walshes.

Using her sleeve, Bell knocked away the remaining jagged pieces and reached her arm through the opening. She groped for the door handle and came up several inches short.

"Hold on. My arms are longer than yours."

She stood aside for Gardy, who pushed his arm through the missing pane. He grunted, straining to reach the handle. With his arm at full extension, his fingers fell short of the mark by a few inches.

Now Lerner climbed the steps and stared incredulously at the agents.

"Are the two of you satisfied?"

"Smile, Sheriff. Thanks to Agent Bell and her somewhat unconventional techniques, we're several steps closer to catching the killer."

"How is that?"

"Unless our murderer's arms stretch to his ankles, there's no way he could have put his hand through and unlocked the door."

"Meaning?"

Bell folded her arms and leaned against the rail.

"The killer was inside the house the whole time. How in the hell did I miss it?"

Lerner's eyes traveled between the opening and the handle.

"Wait just a second. Let me try."

The agents moved aside as the sheriff waddled forward. He had a confident look in his eyes, a certainty he'd prove the woman wrong. The agents shared a grin as he struggled to reach the lock. He was red-faced and out of breath when he finally pulled his arm back.

"I guess I owe the two of you an apology. Let me get

this straight. The killer was already inside the house while the Goodrich boy visited Kacy Deering."

Gardy nodded.

"No doubt he figured Braden Goodrich would give him a fight, so he waited for the boy to leave before he made his move."

"And smashed the pane after the fact to make it look like a break-in. Jesus. I can't believe we didn't see it."

"Which also explains why Kacy didn't hear the killer break into the house," said Bell, pumping with adrenaline now that the puzzle pieces fit together. "He was already upstairs."

A sudden gust nearly stole Lerner's hat. The leaves rattled like dead things.

Gardy descended the stairs and gave the front of the house one last look.

"No other signs of forced entry. I can examine the sides and back, but I won't find anything different from yesterday."

Bell followed Gardy to the sidewalk, the sheriff trailing behind.

"Gardy, who did the Walshes say had keys to the house?"

"Two people. The neighbor, Clyde Sullivan."

"He ain't our guy," said Lerner.

"And the brother who lives in Kalamazoo."

Bell shook her head and paced a trench into the lawn.

"That can't be right, Gardy. They forgot someone."

"I'll give Nathan Walsh a call."

Gardy walked a few paces away. She couldn't eavesdrop on the conversation with Lerner rambling continuous apologies, but Gardy wore a grin when he returned.

"About two years ago Walsh hired a local contractor to redo the basement. A guy named Alan Hodge."

"I know Hodge," Lerner said. "He corners the market on contracting work in Coral Lake."

"They gave him a house key, which he returned, but he could have copied it in the meantime."

The wheels spun faster in Bell's head.

She brought the phone to her ear and listened as it rang and rang.

"Bell?"

She held Gardy's eyes and placed her finger over her lips. Just before she gave up, a voice answered on the other end. Tired, haggard.

"Hello?"

"Mrs. Deering?"

"Hold on…yes…who is this?"

Something toppled over. Deering cursed under her breath. It was clear the woman was three sheets to the wind or hungover.

"Mrs. Deering, this is Agent Bell."

"Agent…Agent Bell. What time is it?"

"Please, Mrs. Deering. I have one quick question to ask. It won't take a moment."

An exasperated groan.

"Fine. Ask away."

"Have you had any repairs done to your house over the last two years?"

"Repairs? What's this about?"

"Think hard."

It was quiet on the other end. Bell wondered if Deering had fallen asleep.

"No, not that I can recall."

Bell's stomach sank. It had to be the handyman. She was sure.

"Are you absolutely certain?"

More silence. Deering coughed, a thick, mucus-filled

hack that made Bell cringe.

"I'm sure. No, the only thing we did was remodel the basement, but it wasn't a repair. I wanted someplace for Kacy and her friends to—"

"Who did the remodel?"

Gardy and Lerner watched Bell, who held up a finger.

When Deering said it was Alan Hodge, Bell snapped her finger and mouthed the handyman's name at Gardy. Already Gardy had his own phone to his ear. She could overhear him trying to find someone at Quantico to run a background check on Hodge.

Bell thanked Deering and ended the call, cutting her off as the woman's questions became frantic. Even in her state of confusion, Deering had seemed to figure out Hodge was a suspect.

"Gee, I don't know about this." Lerner rubbed behind his neck. "Alan Hodge works for half the families in Coral Lake."

"Tell me more about Hodge. Is he a large man?"

"I suppose so. I mean he's maybe an inch or two taller than me."

"But strong."

"Thick, I guess you would say. The guy spends his days carrying washers and dryers down basement stairs."

"And he lives alone. No wife or kids."

"Are you asking me or telling me? Seems like you already have all the answers."

"Sorry, Sheriff. Truthfully, profiles are just theories. They aren't foolproof, and there isn't any guarantee Hodge is our man."

Yet her gut told her otherwise. She hadn't seen a photograph of Hodge, but the picture she'd worked up in her head sent goosebumps down her arms.

Remodels took weeks to complete, sometimes months. A lot of time to observe a teenage girl. That's how the obsession began.

"Understood. To answer your question, yes, Hodge is unmarried. No girlfriend as far as I know, but I can ask around."

"Probably unnecessary. Listen, we think the reason he scalped Kacy and took her clothes is so he can keep her alive, be able to play with her as long as he wants."

Lerner's mouth twisted as if he'd bitten down on something sour.

"But she's dead."

"Yes, but a part of his mind believes otherwise, even though he consciously recognizes it's all fantasy."

"You told us this during the first briefing. I don't see how this helps. The evidence is purely circumstantial, nothing a judge would issue a warrant over without some way to tie him to the scene."

Over Lerner's shoulder, Bell could see Gardy talking into his phone, hand over his other ear to block out the wind.

"It's important because the person who murdered Kacy, be it Hodge or someone else, needs privacy."

"As I confirmed, Hodge lives alone."

"What's his address?"

"Canal Street, right in the center of the village where they're setting up for the strawberry festival. Christ, his house was a stone's throw from us yesterday."

Part of the profile fractured in Bell's head. No, it wasn't likely Hodge kept Kacy's remains in his house. Though he could easily conceal the clothes and hair in a bag, Hodge would want more seclusion. Too many people strolling Canal Street, shopping and glancing through his windows as they passed. It sounded like everyone in town knew him. Plus, and this thought made Bell cringe, the remains would begin to stink and attract attention.

She was about to ask Lerner another question when

Gardy walked over, the phone back in his pocket.

"So Alan Hodge grew up in two different foster homes, the first in the northeastern corner of Pennsylvania, the last in Irondequoit outside Rochester. Nothing out of the ordinary we found about the Pennsylvania location. An older couple raised Hodge until he was five, but they gave him up after the father died and the mother fell ill."

An abusive childhood stood center in Bell's pattern. Although multiple foster homes pointed at a disjointed upbringing, it didn't imply maltreatment.

"What about the next family?"

"Not a family. One woman: Rhonda Winston. Turns out the police were called to her house on three separate occasions for suspected abuse, but none of the charges stuck. The catch is Winston was arrested for heroin possession after Hodge turned eighteen and moved. While the officers searched the premises, they discovered a cramped crawlspace in the basement with a dirty cot shoved inside. A couple of children's toys, as well."

"My God."

"Bell, there were leather straps on the side of the cot. Looked like she tied the boy down and locked him inside the crawlspace."

The image came unbidden to her. The filthy cot, probably dotted with vermin droppings. A bare bulb swinging like a hangman. Darkness. His mother's abusive screams. Insanity.

Even Lerner slumped his shoulders as though struck. Bell sifted through the scope of the abuse. Was he beaten? Molested? The background fit. Explained how Hodge's fantasies began and why he needed to be alone with the victim.

"It's him. It has to be Hodge."

"There's something else." Apprehension crawled on centipede legs down Bell's spine. "Rhonda Winston went missing two weeks ago."

"He killed the mother."

"We don't know that."

Yet they did. It was plain on Gardy's face as they walked back to the vehicles. Bell was right about the killer just getting started, except Kacy Deering was his second victim.

"Sheriff," Gardy said, climbing into the Accord. "Call the station and dig up anything you can on Alan Hodge. Bell's right about the need for privacy. Does he have a shop or warehouse he works out of?"

"Good question. I'll have Crandall check the village records."

"Do that, and get back to me as soon as you find something."

"Where are you going?"

"Hodge's house."

Gardy shifted into drive. The sheriff yelled something over the engine noise about not having a warrant. Bell's hands trembled as the Accord hugged the curves of Coral Hill.

CHAPTER FOURTEEN

"It can't be in the center of the village. Hodge has to work in privacy."

The road flew at the windshield as Bell clutched her phone and waited for Lerner to reply. She heard the sheriff shuffe papers, then fingers clacked away on a keyboard.

The village was lit in orange as the sun descended into Coral Lake. The car lurched to a stop at a red light.

"Just go through," she mouthed to Gardy. But he couldn't. A train of pedestrians was crossing in front of him. "Come on, Sheriff. There has to be something."

Lerner's voice warbled through the speaker.

"Nothing yet, but...hold on, I've got Crandall on the other line."

Bell watched the houses move by slower now. Gardy had turned off the main road onto Canal Street. A scattering of modest and upscale homes lined the road. Lawns were well kept, the landscaping manicured. Hodge's home was the third property from the corner. It was a small, white two-story, so nondescript it appeared to hide in plain sight. A short concrete walkway led to a set of gray stairs. A screened-in porch fronted the door. Through the screen's haze Bell could see a rocking chair, table, and what appeared to be the remnants of an old washing machine.

The car hadn't come to a complete stop when Bell threw open the door. Gardy snagged her shirt before she could jump.

"Will you slow down?"

"We both know it's Hodge."

"And we don't have a warrant, not even probable cause to search the house."

She threw Gardy's hand off her shoulder.

"He might be killing her right now. I'll take my chances on—"

Lerner's voice cut her off. She'd forgotten about him.

"Repeat, Sheriff."

"Agent Bell, I just got off the phone with Deputy Crandall. He says Hodge owns land on the west side of the lake. A half-mile north of the Jepsen-Burns interchange. There are about four square miles of undeveloped land, mostly used by the locals for nature walks and hiking. Hodge's property sits about a hundred yards above the lake."

She scrolled through a GPS map until she found the interchange. She followed the map northward and saw the forest. Her heart drummed harder.

"I see it."

"Good. Because we can move on him now. One of Angela Thiele's coworkers recognized Hodge's van at the pharmacy last night. Says she only noticed because he was parked in the employee's section, right up against Thiele's Rogue."

"To prevent her from opening the door."

"Right. The girl went inside to tell Angela how close the van was to her father's vehicle, just in case Hodge scratched it, but Angela was already gone."

A shiver rolled through Bell. There was a good chance Angela was already inside Hodge's van when the coworker noticed. It was a small measure of luck he hadn't captured the other girl, too.

"Someone recognized Hodge's van parked beside Angela at the pharmacy last night," she said to Gardy.

Gardy cocked his head out the window and examined the empty driveway.

"That qualifies as probable cause in my book. I don't see his van, though."

"He's not here, Gardy. Hodge owns undeveloped land on the west side of the lake."

"Do we have an address?"

"Working on that right now."

Setting the GPS to the approximate coordinates of Hodge's forestland, Bell pressed start and read the directions.

"We're sending two cars to his place on Canal Street," Lerner said. She'd sent his voice through the car speakers so they could both listen.

"That's fine, Sheriff," said Gardy, wheeling the Accord around. "But I seriously doubt he's here."

"I'll have my men check the house regardless and meet you on the west side of the lake. I already put a bulletin out for Hodge's van."

"Good work, Sheriff. We'll be there in five."

Gardy took the corner hard into the village center. Darkness descended on the village as the Accord motored toward the west side of the lake.

CHAPTER FIFTEEN

The footsteps were right behind Angela as she struggled down the hill. She thought she could outrun Hodge, but he was faster than she believed possible as he hurtled down the hill on momentum.

He tackled her in the grass, and the ropes sprang apart. Her hands free, she jumped to her feet before he collapsed down on her.

His fingers grasped her hair, and she spun and slapped his hands away. She backed up and lost her footing. Struck the ground. Her vision went blurry as the air whistled out of her lungs.

He pounced on her, all girth and muscle. One hand gripped her neck as the other cocked back in a fist. She bridged hard and jabbed her fingers into his eyes.

Still straddling her stomach, Hodge yelled and grasped his face. Angela bridged again and twisted, and this time Hodge rolled off. As she climbed to her feet and ran for the road, he blindly swiped his hand out and clutched her ankle. She screamed and fell. The road was so close. Only fifty feet away. If anyone drove past, they'd see the struggle and come to her aid. But there was nobody. Just the empty clearing and the growing darkness. And Hodge's insane bellowing.

Angela felt herself dragged backward. He still had one hand around her ankle. The other massaged his eyes. He was too strong. No way she could kick free.

Instead, she allowed Hodge to drag her, and when he was close, she kicked her free foot into his groin and toppled him.

The bastard refused to release his grip. She yelled for help and slammed the back of her other foot down on his hand. And again. This time his hand opened, and she scurried away as he lay curled on the ground.

Angela willed her legs to work. Her knees kept folding when she tried to stand. He came after her on all fours. Called her *traitor*. Promised she would pay for turning on him, for abandoning Kacy.

The starlit lake was just below the road. The water called to her. So many fond memories were tied to the lake. Boating with her parents when she was a child. Skipping school on the first warm day of spring with Terri, letting the sun bake their bikini-clad bodies. The timeline of her life was tied to watching the sun rise and set over this lake.

She couldn't die here. Wouldn't allow him to take her life.

So she crawled faster as he closed the distance between them. The ground cut into her bare knees, scraped at her palms.

A strange mantra played around in her head. If she could make it to the lake, everything would be okay. Hope buoyed when she heard the approaching engine.

She was a few feet from the road when his hands closed around her neck.

CHAPTER SIXTEEN

Bell unbuckled the seatbelt and leaned forward. A loaded spring ready to explode. Gardy sneaked a glance at her, but the tree-lined road accelerated at the windshield and forced him to focus on driving.

In the headlight beams she saw the trail branch off to the right.

"There! I see it."

He slammed the brakes and fishtailed the Accord. The path came up on them too fast, forcing Gardy to back up and yank hard on the steering wheel to make the turn.

The car jounced over rocks and miniature hillocks as it climbed. Trees leaned over the trail. In the dark they appeared as deformed beasts, their branches claws that would rake Bell's eyes out when she exited the vehicle.

Lerner's voice came through the speakers. The sheriff was halfway to the village and would reach their location in fifteen minutes.

Bell rolled down the window and leaned her head out. She searched for any indication of Hodge's lair. It had to be here somewhere. This was where he took the girls.

"We'll find her," Gardy said.

The Accord hugged a hard curve. The spike strips

vaulted out of the ground.

Gardy braked too late. The jagged teeth tore into the tires with shotgun pops. Momentum jerked the back end of the car toward the forest. Then they shot sideways down the incline. The trees rushing at them. Gardy pulling on the wheel.

The driver side barreled into the trees. An awful crunch of metal and glass.

Gardy's head struck the window and ricocheted. She watched his eyes roll back into his skull as the seatbelt clutched his shoulder and neck.

It was quiet now. The radio was dead. Night sounds swelled around the vehicle.

Bell tried to rouse him, but Gardy didn't respond. She didn't dare touch him. Worried over spinal injuries. His neck lolled over against a backdrop of crumpled glass. To her relief he breathed.

Her door was jammed. She needed to force it open with her shoulder, but when she stepped down it felt as if someone drove a lance through her knee.

Bell's legs buckled. She leaned on all fours. Bloody drool trickled off her lips, and she swiped it away with her hand.

Trembling, she struggled to her feet and limped a few inches at a time until her knee reluctantly agreed to support her weight. She walked in absolute darkness and searched for the trail.

"I'm coming back for you," she promised the man in the car. "I'll get help."

Gardy didn't respond. She watched him in silhouette, slumped over and lifeless, a marionette propped up by the seatbelt. It killed her to leave him, but she had to find Angela.

She flicked on her handheld radio to dead silence. Broken. When that failed she used her phone to dial the sheriff's number. It took several rings before he answered.

"Lerner?"

"That you, Agent Bell?"

"I need an ambulance. Agent Gardy's hurt."

He stammered over the growl of his engine. If she used her imagination, she thought she heard the Ram's motor on the ridge. He couldn't be more than ten minutes away.

"Shit. Okay, stay calm. Are you injured?"

"I'm fine. Just get help for Gardy."

She'd wandered up the trail for over a minute when she saw the wooden bulk of the shed growing out of the earth. She threw herself inside the shadow of an elm tree.

It was dark inside the shed, no hint of light bleeding around the door. Her hand moved to her hip and removed the Glock-22.

She was breathing too fast. Getting lightheaded. The night seemed to swallow everything except the shed as she cautiously approached.

With her back against the wall, she reached for the door latch. Counted to three while muttering a prayer inside her head.

Bell whipped open the door and spun into the entryway, gun raised. The dark rolled out to greet her. Darkness and a carrion scent.

She turned on the flashlight and saw the girl on the cot. A teenager. Stiff. Rigor mortis already setting in. Her heart fell before she inched forward and saw it was a mannequin. In the gloom it looked real. The little girl inside her worried the mannequin would suddenly sit up.

Swiping the light around, she stared at the blood-smeared pelt atop its head. Kacy. Her stomach turned.

Leather straps hung off the cot. Hodge had recreated his nightmarish childhood.

The shed was otherwise empty. Just the cot and a single bulb affixed to the ceiling. Wires ran through the roof, undoubtedly to a solar panel. A generator would make too much noise and attract attention.

So where were Angela and Hodge?

A flare of hope told her Angela escaped and Hodge was in pursuit. If so they could be anywhere in the forest. Bell forced herself to admit she needed help. The area was too large to canvas by herself, and her knee seemed to be held together by frayed strings.

In the corner lay a toolbox. Peeking her head through the entryway, she confirmed the clearing was empty and closed the door.

Bell opened the toolbox and removed the top compartment. Beneath lay a stack of photographs. She thumbed through the candid pictures of Kacy and Angela, some apparently taken inside the girls' homes while Hodge worked. And another girl, a pretty teen Bell didn't recognize. His next target.

She closed the shed. The forest thickened behind the shed where Hodge's land ended. The trail led back to the road and lake. Somewhere along the way was the Accord. And Gardy.

Fireflies ignited the air as she walked, keeping to the grass in case Hodge was watching the trail. Help was late in arriving. Bell should have heard Lerner's truck by now.

A cool wind blew off the lake, whipping at her face and making it difficult to discern noises. Whispering another promise to help Gardy, she made it back to the road and knelt amid an overgrowth of weed and grasses.

His footsteps approached before she swung around with the gun.

Hodge struck her from behind and sent her reeling. She fell forward as he drove his weight down on her back. The overgrowth claimed the gun and hid it from Bell as she desperately groped through the darkness.

His hands clutched her neck and squeezed. Reaching up, she grabbed the back of his head and tried to flip him over. Hodge was too strong. He muscled his neck backward and broke her grip, then he rose and crashed down on her spine, driving the air from her lungs.

She coughed and sucked the night air into her chest. Bell ran her legs along the ground and attempted to squirm out from underneath. His hands closed around her neck again. The thick meat of his fingertips dug into her windpipe while he thrust down on the small of her back.

Then he clutched her by the hair and drove her face into the dirt. Ripped her head up and smashed it down again.

Blood poured from her nose. She tasted it on her lips.

He lifted her head and drove it into the ground again, this time grinding her face into the earth.

Toying with her.

She strained her back trying to rise. His weight was fully upon her, making it impossible to throw him off.

The terrain spun when he resumed choking her. A terrible wheeze came from her throat when she tried to inhale. Her vision failed as she started to lose consciousness.

He crept higher up her back. Increasing his leverage, she knew. Bell used the opportunity to crawl onto her knees.

She would die if she didn't free herself in the next few seconds. Unable to breathe, she felt the fight drain out of her. She bent forward and whipped her head back. It struck Hodge's face flush. His grip weakened, yet he continued to strangle her. Bell cracked her head against his face again, and Hodge fell backward holding his nose.

Blood gushed between his fingers as Bell croaked and coughed. She couldn't suck the air back into her lungs quickly enough.

Pins-and-needles coursed through her arms as she struggled onto all fours. He rose behind her as she forced herself to crawl into the road.

The macadam dug into her knees. Ahead, the lake sloshed against the shoreline. She imagined the sheriff's truck coming around the bend and cutting her in half as she continued to crawl. Her will to survive kept her from fainting, wouldn't allow her to stop.

Hodge caught her in the road. He booted Bell in the ribs and crumpled her. She curled up as he kicked her again, the impact driving spikes of pain through her ribcage. She swiped at his leg, but he had her by the hair now. Pulling her across the blacktop. Dragging her over the gravel shoulder toward the water.

Bell felt the rocky shoreline scrape her back before she knew where she was. Hodge stood over her, ripping the hair from her scalp and leering. He flung her into the shallows where something sharp and rusted sliced into her shoulder. The blade of an abandoned outboard motor.

She saw a darker pool well up through the ripples. Her blood. It poured out of the open wound.

He clutched her from behind. The muscles of his forearms closed over her windpipe in a headlock. She whipped her head backward, but he was ready this time and moved his bloodied face away. He grabbed her by the hair and shoved her face underwater. Her hands slid across slick stones and plunged into the mud.

Bell's legs flailed as he drowned her. She closed her hand over a rock, searching for something large enough. The fist-sized stone was smooth and round. It kept slipping from her hands as she tried to grasp hold. Water filled her lungs. She wretched as he yanked her head back by the hair, coughing out muddy lake water.

When Hodge shoved her head under she swung back with the rock. She struck his face, but there was no leverage behind the blow. The rock glanced harmlessly off his cheek and dropped from her hand as she imagined him laughing.

He pushed Bell's face into the muddy lake bottom. Muck filled her mouth and eyes, her legs coming to rest behind him as her life teetered.

Hodge tugged Bell out of the water and sat on the small of her back. Clutching her chin from behind with both hands, he leaned back and strained to snap her neck. Her spine shrieked with pain.

The agony flared her senses, her body breaking.

When Hodge leaned farther backward he lost his grip, his slick fingers sliding off her chin. She twisted beneath him, drove her palm up, and struck his shattered nose. A sound like twigs snapping.

Stunned, Hodge stumbled backward. He quickly shook the cobwebs out and came at her.

Bell flipped over and scissored her legs around his neck as he leaned down. His eyes went wide as her thighs clamped together. Straining, squeezing until her legs shook.

He went down to one knee, and she thought she had him. Then he pushed up and lifted Bell's entire body off the ground. Clutching her hips, he tried to throw her down.

She refused to let go. Veins stood out down his neck and arms. He beat his fists against her thighs. Lifted her higher.

He almost had her over his head when she jerked her back and twisted. A crackle as the torque snapped his neck.

Hodge went limp. They crashed to the ground together. Bell landed on Hodge's legs.

She rolled off and lay on her back. Hodge's eyes were open but blank. The man appeared to be stargazing, except his chest no longer moved.

Carefully, she moved her palm over his face and thought this is the part of the movie when the killer suddenly opens his eyes and sits up.

Thankfully, he didn't. Bell was too exhausted to defend herself if he did.

She tried to crawl into a sitting position and collapsed. Her shirt was soaked with blood, the shoulder wound shooting waves of hot pain down her arm.

A moment later, she heard the motor approach. Lerner to the rescue. Bell's eyes squinted shut. Through tears, she began to laugh.

CHAPTER SEVENTEEN

Gardy was somewhere near the lake shore. The starlight was sharp, the moon coloring the water an eerie blue-gray.

He'd come awake minutes ago and stumbled through the trees before he shook the dust out of his brain and realized he was lost. The girl's cry snapped him awake, and he followed the voice, calling out to her every minute until he zeroed in on her location.

He was somewhere south of Hodge's property when he saw Angela Thiele splayed over the rocks. Her legs extended into the lake up to her knees. Waves rolled over her stomach and splashed her face. She cried harder when she saw him. It wasn't until then he realized how terrifying he must have looked. A helmet of blood-soaked hair, a leaking gash on his forehead, eyes glowing in the moonlight. His badge was on crooked. At least that was an easy fix.

Realizing who he was, the girl calmed.

Gardy didn't know much about lakes or if tide played a factor, but it was plain the waves were getting higher as the wind gusted toward the shoreline. Soon the water would be over Angela's head.

"Don't worry, Angela. You're safe now. I'll get you back to your parents. Are you injured?"

She shook her head. That was a good sign. He prompted the girl to move her arms, then her legs. Not paralyzed, just exhausted and in a state of shock.

Everything hurt when he knelt down. He slipped one arm under her neck, the other beneath her knees, and scooped her up. Water poured off her body as he carried her up the shoreline and toward the road. He almost missed the two silhouettes strewn across the shore a quarter-mile away. Jesus, Bell.

He walked in Bell's direction, the girl waterlogged and limp as a rag doll in his arms, when he heard the ghost screams. Coming closer. Tired and confused, he took a while to figure out the wailing ghost was an ambulance siren, then the truck's headlights flared over the hill and lit his face. Gently setting the girl down, he waved his arms until the sheriff swerved in his direction and stopped along the shoulder.

The look on Lerner's face was one of abject horror as he climbed down from the cab. The ambulance came to a stop behind Lerner's truck as Gardy leaned over, hands on knees.

A female paramedic with blue eyes and a lion's mane of blonde hair tried to stop Gardy as he limped past.

"Agent?"

Gardy looked over his shoulder at Lerner.

"I'll live. Take care of the girl. I'm going after Bell."

***

Bell's eyes shot open at the sound of footsteps. Thinking it was Hodge, her hand instinctively moved to her hip for the missing gun.

She saw Gardy and gasped. The shock of his

bloodied forehead didn't last long before her eyes turned cross.

"Just like you to show up in the nick of time and save the day."

He dropped to one knee, saw Hodge's crumpled form and reached for his gun. She snickered, though doing so quickly reminded her how much she hurt.

"Don't worry, Superman, I already defeated the villain."

A beam of red light rotated over their heads. She could hear Lerner's voice and two others, probably emergency workers. As he ran his eyes over her wounds, he stopped on the empty holster.

"And you lost your gun again, I see. Weber will be thrilled."

"Weber can…ow!"

She flinched when he touched her shoulder. Gardy issued a sharp whistle that momentarily deafened her. He waved someone forward, and she heard footsteps approaching.

The sudden memory of why they were on Hodge's property jolted her. She tried to sit up. Gardy blocked her from doing so.

"Where's the girl? Is Angela alive?

"She's fine, Bell." She held his eyes and searched for a flicker of dishonesty. "I swear to you. She's in the ambulance by now. You'll meet her at the hospital."

"I don't need to go the hospital. Help me up."

"You do and you will," Gardy said as the blonde paramedic stooped beside him. He met the woman's eyes and cocked his head at Bell. "She's stubborn, this one. Good luck."

The woman took one look at Bell's shoulder and winced.

"Ma'am, I need you to remain still. I'm going to cut

away the fabric and dress that wound."

Bell rolled her eyes.

"You know how much I paid for this shirt?" She saw Gardy raise an eyebrow and scowled. "Fine. It was on the Target clearance rack. Still nice, though and...ouch! Are you sure you need to do that?"

Placing gauze over the wound, the woman pressed down.

"Just to stop the bleeding. With how long you've been bleeding, I'm surprised you're conscious."

"Feel free to put her under," Gardy said. The paramedic didn't seem to hear him. "I'm a little jealous of that injury, Bell."

Bell glared at him and sucked air through her teeth when the pressure increased.

"What the hell are you talking about?"

"That'll leave a nice little scar. You can't buy street cred like that."

CHAPTER EIGHTEEN

An endless ocean of blue flowed outside the plane's windows. Bell stretched her aching legs and leaned the seat back, muttering a silent prayer of thanks that the return trip to Dulles had remained smooth. Gardy sat in the next seat and sifted through the case notes, a thick eye-patch-looking bandage affixed to his forehead that made him look like a pirate with bad aim.

The flight attendant was a male this time, and to Bell's boundless amusement, he paid Gardy an uncanny amount of attention. He brought the agent another tea when Bell elbowed him.

"Bet he's a Pisces."

"I bet you should shut up."

The flight attendant gave them a curious glance. Bell grinned.

"Don't worry. Inside joke."

She reached for her iPad and groaned, forgetting the shoulder.

"Serves you right for making fun of him. He's just being friendly."

"He's being more than friendly, Gardy. You see, this is why you can't get a date. Women throw you signals all the time and they go straight over your head. Besides, I wasn't making fun of him. That would be rude." She shifted the ice pack on her shoulder. "I was making fun of you."

Bell's stomach dropped when the plane unexpectedly began its descent. She blew the hair from her eyes.

"Maybe I should fly back to Coral Lake," she said.

Gardy unfolded a pair of reading glasses and set them on the end of his nose, jotting something down as he watched her from the corner of his eye.

"Need a vacation?"

"My parents are coming for the week."

"That's wonderful. You didn't tell me your parents were visiting. When do I get to say hello?"

"I'll let them know how excited you are to meet them. Hey, I've got a great idea. Maybe they can stay at your place."

"The bachelor pad? That would kill my swagger, Special Agent Bell." When she didn't laugh, he put down the pen and peered at her through the tops of his eyes. "Okay, what's bugging you?"

Bell shook her head and stared out the window.

"They're okay, but I can't deal with the *I-told-you-so* lectures right now."

"How do you mean?"

"That I'd just get hurt working this crazy job. This *man's* job. Dad always figured me for an exciting career in the retail industry. Or maybe I'd be a fashion designer."

"Nothing wrong with fashion design."

"Didn't say there was. My college roommate makes six figures in fashion design. I can't wait until Mom and Dad see my shoulder. Wouldn't be surprised if they end up in Weber's office Monday morning and berate him for putting their precious daughter in danger. My parents are good people, but their expertise is in running my life."

Gardy removed another folder from his briefcase and

thumbed through a series of notes and photographs.

"You tend to exaggerate when things don't go your way. I'm positive it's not as bad as it sounds."

"Well, you say that now, but wait until they try to fix us up."

Gardy coughed into his hand. The male flight attendant was quick to ensure he was okay.

The plane was ten minutes from arrival when Bell glanced over and saw the photograph.

Logan Wolf.

She'd recognize the deep-set, black eyes anywhere. They seemed to penetrate her mind.

"New evidence?"

Gardy flipped to a map of the United States. A scattering of dots indicated where Wolf was recently seen.

"Tough to say. There was a murder outside of Melbourne, Florida last week. A drifter. Officially, it's an unsolved murder, but the MO looks like Wolf's work."

Victim's throat slashed with a sack over his head. Seven such murders in the last year alone.

She wondered if anyone would ever find Logan Wolf, the former BAU-agent-turned-serial-killer. A master profiler, Wolf returned home from work one night in July of 2013 and butchered his wife. Throat slashed. Sack over her head. There was never an explanation. Wolf simply vanished.

Bell shivered. The perfect killer. Impossible to catch.

"Oh, we'll catch him," Gardy said, reading her face. "He might cover his tracks better than the Alan Hodges of the world, but he can't hide forever."

"He's been doing a good job so far."

Gardy slid the folder into his briefcase and locked it away.

Bell didn't look forward to landing. She could have stayed in the air for another month. Between her parents and Weber, Bell didn't relish facing the new week. After the

Deputy Director saw their injuries and figured out she'd lost her gun, he'd have a conniption.

Gardy closed his eyes. Bell was about to do the same when the male flight attendant smiled and handed her a business card. She turned it over and grinned. When the attendant disappeared toward the back of the plane, Bell slipped the card into Gardy's pocket.

His eyes sprang open and glanced down at his open pocket.

"What was that?"

"Smile, Gardy. He gave you his phone number."

***

Ready for the next Scarlett Bell thriller?
Order Book 2 - Blood Storm today!

CHAPTER NINETEEN

FREE PREVIEW
OF
BLOOD STORM

Cars hurtle past Clarice, their taillights painting red streaks across her eyes. Stereos thump bass, and she can feel it in her chest. In the distance, the neon lights of countless tourist shops burn brightly.

She has walked for almost an hour now. Lost and afraid. Feet ache. The discount heels aren't helping matters.

The late summer heat is a second skin she can't peel off. It weighs her down. Slumps her back and makes her knees heavy.

As she passes a vacant storefront, she sees her reflection in the glass—the dark, curly hair matted to her head as the sweat pours off in buckets.

The sun is below the ground now, the blues and magentas of gloaming rapidly draining to black. She sneaks a glance over her shoulder but no one is following. Just her mind playing tricks on her, turning every shadow malevolent.

She abandoned her car after the temperature light spiked and steam rolled out of the hood. Of course, the phone is dead. Damn battery drains if she looks at it wrong.

Clarice stumbles through the wrong side of Sunset Island and thinks she knows where she is. If she is correct about her location, the boardwalk is only five blocks away. There the lights will be bright, the streets lined with vacationing families. Safety. Someone will help her.

The faraway blinking lights become a beacon. They pull her forward and make her legs not so weary. She will be all right.

A dark sedan slows to a stop, and a man leans his head through the passenger window. Another man sits behind the wheel. She considers asking them for a ride before she notices the passenger leering at her. A catcall. For a second, Clarice thinks she hears the door latch opening, then the car spins its screeching tires and jets up the road.

She brushes the sweat off her forehead and moves off the sidewalk and into the grass. Slips off her shoes. Ahead lies a vacant parking lot of shattered glass and oil residue, but she takes advantage of the grass while she can, the soft carpet heaven under her feet.

Clarice is almost to the parking lot when she hears the big truck motor crawl up from behind. She walks a little faster, and the truck keeps pace. It's a rusted, shabby Ford F-150. A dark color she can't make out in the failing light. It follows along, falling behind then jerking forward. Her heart is in her throat when the motor guns and the truck disappears into the night.

Except that it doesn't disappear. After she slips her shoes on and hurries across the parking lot, she sees the truck pulled to the side of the road. The engine is off, the dead-eye taillights extinguished. She looks for a side street, an alternative route that avoids the truck. There is none. It's either go forward or turn around and risk the rundown section of Sunset Island again.

As Clarice approaches the truck she doesn't see the driver. The windows are tinted but she can see a vague outline of the steering column. She breathes faster when she is even with the bumper, head on a swivel. A row of houses sprout up around her. Though many are derelict with sagging porches and broken windows, she takes solace that the worst of the resort city is behind her.

She is almost to the end of the block when she sees the man behind the hedgerow. He watches her approach, then steps back into the shadow and vanishes. It could be anyone, she thinks. A homeowner. Someone who might call a tow truck or drive her to the boardwalk. Her intuition tells her otherwise. It's the truck driver. She senses him.

The darkness is almost complete when she stops. Perhaps the best course of action is to turn around and wait until she is sure the man is gone.

No, he will still be here no matter how late the hour is when she returns.

She veers off the sidewalk before she reaches the hedgerow, intending to cross the street, when the shadow breaks out from the bushes. He'd been standing beside her the whole time without her noticing.

Before she can scream, he covers her mouth and clamps a forearm over her chest. As she flails in his grip the man drags her into the bushes. Thorns reach out and tear her skin. Clarice bites down on his hand, the only defense she can think of, and the man hisses.

Then anguish as he strikes her in the back of the neck. A club of some sort. She pitches forward onto her knees and he clubs her again. The world spins as she splays out on her stomach. She feels a hot trickle of blood on the back of her head and neck and knows she must remain conscious if she is to survive.

Clutching at clumps of grass, she drags herself

forward. Across the lawn of the unlit residence. Somewhere a box air conditioner rattles, and another vehicle passes. Nobody sees or bothers to help.

He follows her. She sees his shadow enveloping her own, a predator stalking wounded prey.

The man grunts and brings the club down on her head again. Her eyes flutter shut.

She can feel his hand around her ankle, grass and stone under her stomach as he drags her deeper into the darkness.

And then she feels nothing at all.

CHAPTER TWENTY

Lightning stroked across the sky as Special Agent Scarlett Bell gripped the steering wheel and fought to keep the Accord in its lane. Her partner, Neil Gardy, sat in the next seat, one eye on the darkening sky and the other on the case briefing.

She wasn't dressed for South Carolina heat. The pant suit itched and made her dread what it would feel like on the beach. What she wouldn't have done to pull her blonde hair back in a ponytail, trade the suit for shorts and a tank, and spend the afternoon in the hotel pool.

"That hurricane isn't headed this way, is it?"

Gardy checked his phone.

"Nope. The National Hurricane Center predicts landfall over Central Georgia in the next 24 hours."

"Still, that's a little close for comfort."

They'd attended a conference in Savannah and received a call about a dismembered body on Sunset Island, South Carolina, a narrow strip of land which curled into the Atlantic and drew tourists from as far away as Maine and Quebec. The barrier island barely jutted above sea level, a sitting duck in a storm surge. Were it not for the traffic the drive would have taken only a half-hour.

A sudden gust of wind pulled the car out of its lane into oncoming cars. A chorus of horns squawked as Bell righted the vehicle.

Breathing heavily, both eyes glued to the road, she wondered why he'd insisted on renting another Accord.

"Boy, I'd love to drive an SUV right now. One of those over-sized monsters that stand up to hurricanes, tornadoes, and New Jersey drivers."

Gardy gave his trademark snicker, the one that reminded her of Muttley, the cartoon dog. He sneered at her and flipped between grisly photographs of a murdered woman.

"I tried, but they were out. Besides, nothing stands up to New Jersey drivers."

"I think you wanted the Accord. It was all part of your evil plan. Do you own stock in Honda?"

As fast as the storm had formed, it split apart and died. Typical southeastern summer weather. One second a raging typhoon soaked you to the bone, the next it was sunny.

And perpetually humid. Even with the windows rolled up and the air conditioner on, Bell couldn't stop sweating.

They were five minutes from where the body had been found on the beach. A woman, dismembered and buried in the sand.

"Our contact is Detective Joe McKenna," Gardy said, closing up the folder and cracking the window open. He looked a little green. "He's leading the investigation."

Gardy burped into his hand. Bell glanced at her partner.

"Don't tell me you're carsick."

"I shouldn't read while the car is moving."

"I'll slow down."

"No, just get us there. I'll feel better once I get out and walk."

Getting there proved to be problematic. The train of vehicles nearly came to a stop, edging forward, bumper-to-bumper as horns honked. Welcome to paradise. Bell saw the toll booths a half-mile up the road. Only two booths, hardly enough to handle peak season traffic.

Bell tapped a drumbeat on the steering wheel.

"You know what this reminds me of?"

"The traffic? I'd say D.C. during the morning rush. Or Beirut."

"No, the case. You remember the Cleveland Torso Murderer?"

"Vaguely. That was the 1930s, right? Something close to twenty dismembered bodies, but they never found the killer. A little before my time."

"You sure about that?"

He snickered again, and as she glanced over she detected fewer flecks of gray dotting his dark, brown hair.

"Agent Gardy, are you coloring your hair?"

"What? No…I…uh…"

"Uh-huh."

He craned his neck out the window as if a secret route existed around the traffic.

"It's been almost two hours since they found the body," he said, checking his watch. "By the time we get there—"

"I know, I know. I'm trying."

After several minutes of vehicles cutting each other off and drivers shouting lewd insults, they broke free of the glut. The way forward opened to a thoroughfare lined by palm trees and stores painted in bright pastel tones, as the Atlantic sloshed to both sides of the road. For a while, Bell felt a strange sense of vertigo as if she stood upon a monstrous ship, the suggestion of movement beneath as the sun sparkled off the water. She didn't drive so much as the ocean pulled her forward.

The spell broke when the island widened and the thoroughfare dumped them into the heart of the tourist district. Surf shops and seafood restaurants. A few boutique hotels nestled between ice cream stands and arcades. The license plates represented the entire east coast and some from as far away as California and Texas. The largest hotels grew against a tropical blue sky. The ocean thrashed behind the concrete structures.

Gardy's color improved the moment they stepped out of the car, and he immediately slipped on a pair of sunglasses as the glare intensified.

"Feeling better now?"

"Much better, thanks. But I should probably drive on the way back."

She tossed him the keys. He caught them one-handed and slipped them into his pocket.

"Show off."

Bell saw the crowd massing around the scene when they reached the beach. Yellow police tape stretched between roadblocks and flapped in the wind, the barrier holding back a curious throng. A few people held their phones over their heads and snapped photographs while a row of police officers urged them back.

A tall officer with cropped black hair held up his hand when Gardy and Bell approached. Gardy flashed his badge, and the cop nodded and waved them through.

Halfway between the looky-loos and the body, a middle-aged detective in a white Polo shirt jogged forward to meet them.

"You must be the agents from the Behavioral Analysis Unit."

"I'm Agent Gardy, and this is Agent Bell."

"Joe McKenna," the detective said, shaking Gardy's hand first, then Bell's. "Glad you could come on short notice. How was traffic on the way in?"

"Stop-and-go."

"You're lucky," McKenna said, walking. "This time of year, it's a lot more stop than go. Anyhow, thanks for giving us a hand. This caught us off guard, and frankly, we don't know what we're up against."

Bell glanced at the crowd and pulled out her phone in case the killer was among the onlookers. Gardy saw her taking photos and gave her a thumbs-up.

A freshly excavated hole lay twenty yards from the water. A pale hand poked into the sun.

Three crime scene techs in white suits finished collecting evidence and packed up their gear. Baggies covered their shoes. Bell wondered how they could walk on the sand dressed like that.

"Around one o'clock this afternoon we received a call about a human hand buried in the sand. A nine-year-old girl was digging around and found it. Fortunately, she didn't find the rest of the body."

Bell grimaced.

"I hope the kid is okay."

"The mother noticed what it was and pulled the girl away before she saw too much. To be perfectly honest, the mother is the one who'll probably end up with nightmares."

"Do we have an ID on the vic?"

"Nothing yet, but I'm confident we'll find out soon. Carlton Yates is the best ME in South Carolina."

A female officer leaned in and said something to McKenna.

"That's fine, Suarez. I'll have the agents examine the body, then we'll clean the scene up." The female officer angled toward the onlookers as McKenna walked beside the agents. "Second body we've found like this, both dismembered, though the last was five years ago. The mayor is having a shit-fit. Not exactly good for the tourist trade when someone's kid digs up body parts. Whatever insight you can lend is most appreciated."

Bell knelt down and covered her mouth. The smell was terrible, a salty carrion stench that steamed out of the hole. Tiny crabs skittered over the scattered body parts, which were roughly arranged to resemble a human.

"Was the previous body found on the beach? The one from five years ago?"

"No. That one was found at a construction site five blocks south of the beach. Assuming it's the same guy, is it normal for a killer to go inactive for five years?"

Bell glanced up at McKenna.

"It's not unheard of. Serial killers change their patterns for reasons we don't fully understand. Some target the same type of victim for years, often a woman who reminds him of someone important from his childhood, then completely shift gears for no apparent reason and track different women. Some kill on a set schedule, others need an outside trigger to set them off. In short, they make their own rules."

"To complicate things further," Gardy said, slipping on a pair of latex gloves. "Maybe the unknown subject spent time in prison. It's not uncommon for a serial killer to have a rap sheet of lesser crimes. The five-year lull might be a clue. I'll have Quantico run a search on anyone from this area who was incarcerated during that time frame."

McKenna nodded absently.

After Bell put on gloves, Gardy manipulated the body. He slipped his hands under the upper torso and tilted it. A dark purple bruise tattooed the woman's neck.

"Blunt force trauma to the back of the neck."

"We saw that, too," McKenna said, wiping his sunglasses on his shirt. "Looks like he struck her with a bat or a rock."

The body was organized like a mad god's doll parts. Four faint purplish tints marked the ankle.

"He dragged her by the ankle," said Bell. "Detective, did the techs dust the ankle for prints?"

"Yeah, but the sand mucked everything up. When we get the body to the coroner's office, we'll take a closer look. They found a blade of grass though."

"Which suggests the body was dumped here."

"That seems likely. We didn't find blood or signs of a struggle nearby, but this stretch of beach is four miles long. Too much area to cover."

The wind gusted and dragged sand across the body. The officers shielded their eyes as children splashed through building waves, oblivious to the macabre scene playing out behind the barricades.

Bell examined the woman's right hand.

"Detective, did you notice the missing forefinger?"

"I meant to ask you about that. We couldn't decide if it was lost in the dismemberment or—"

"No. He took it with him."

Read the next chapter in the Scarlett Bell Serial Killer series. Order Blood Storm on Amazon today.

Let the Party Begin!

I'm a pretty nice guy once you look past the grisly images in my head. Most of all, I love connecting with kickass readers like you.

Join the party and be part of my exclusive VIP Readers Group at:

WWW.DANPADAVONA.COM

Are You a Super Fan?

How would you like to contribute ideas for my next story? Want to read my novels weeks before they are released on Amazon?

Join me on Patreon at https://www.patreon.com/danpadavona for exclusive stories, interviews, video blogs, and general nonsense.

Be a part of my inner circle and team!

Show Your Support for Indie Thriller Authors

Did you enjoy this book? If so, please let other thriller fans know by leaving a short review. Positive reviews help spread the word about independent authors and their novels. Thank you.

Author's Acknowledgment

Mind of a Killer would not be possible without the encouragement, support, and efforts from my patrons.

Lydia Capuano
Tim Feely
Lisa Forlow
Steve Gracin
Michelle Kennedy
Anthony Allen Ratliff
Dawn Spengler

I value each one of you more than I can express.
Thank you for believing in me.

To find out how you can become a patron, please visit me at:

https://www.patreon.com/danpadavona

Why Novellas?

The world of entertainment has changed. While I enjoy movies, I watch Netflix series and comparable programming more frequently. Movies are too short to match the story and character arcs of a well-written series, and that's why I favor a long series of novellas over a few novels.

I prefer a long series which I can lose myself in, but broken up into smaller, manageable episodes that don't take up my entire evening.

In short, I'm writing the types of stories I enjoy and composing them into forms I find preferable.

I sincerely hope you enjoy the Scarlett Bell series as much as I love writing it.

How many episodes can you expect? Provided the series is well-received by readers, I don't foresee a definite end and would prefer to expand on the characters and plot lines for the foreseeable future. I still have plenty of devious ideas for upcoming stories.

Stay tuned!

Mind of a Killer - Paperback

About the Author

Dan Padavona is the author of the The Scarlett Bell thriller series, Severity, The Dark Vanishings series, Camp Slasher, Quilt, Crawlspace, The Face of Midnight, Storberry, Shadow Witch, and the horror anthology, The Island. He lives in upstate New York with his beautiful wife, Terri, and their children, Joe, and Julia. Dan is a meteorologist with NOAA's National Weather Service. Besides writing, he enjoys visiting amusement parks, beach vacations, Renaissance fairs, gardening, playing with the family dogs, and eating ice cream.

Visit Dan at: www.danpadavona.com

Mind of a Killer - Paperback